The Winter's Tale

DOVER · THRIFT · EDITIONS

The Winter's Tale

WILLIAM SHAKESPEARE

DOVER PUBLICATIONS, INC.
Mineola, New York

DOVER THRIFT EDITIONS

GENERAL EDITOR: PAUL NEGRI
EDITOR OF THIS VOLUME: SUSAN L. RATTINER

Bibliographical Note

This Dover edition, first published in 2000, contains the unabridged text of *The Winter's Tale* as published in Volume VIII of *The Caxton Edition of the Complete Works of William Shakespeare*, Caxton Publishing Company, London, n.d. A new introductory Note has been specially prepared for the present edition, and explanatory footnotes from the Caxton edition have been revised.

Library of Congress Cataloging-in-Publication Data

Shakespeare, William, 1564–1616.
    The winter's tale / William Shakespeare.
        p. cm. — (Dover thrift editions)
    Contains the unabridged text of The winter's tale as published in volume VIII of the Caxton edition of the Complete works of William Shakespeare, Caxton Publishing Company, London, n.d., with new introductory note and revised explanatory footnotes.
    ISBN 0-486-41118-4 (pbk.)
      1. Sicily (Italy)—Kings and rulers—Drama. 2. Fathers and daughters—Drama. 3. Married people—Drama. 4. Castaways—Drama. I. Title. II. Series.

PR2839 .A1 2000
822.3'3—dc21

00-027749

Manufactured in the United States of America
Dover Publications, Inc., 31 East 2nd Street, Mineola, N.Y. 11501

Note

ACCORDING TO Simon Forman's *Booke of Plaies and Notes Thereof* (ca. 1611?), the earliest known performance of *The Winter's Tale* took place at the Globe Theatre on May 15, 1611. Already established as a premier writer of tragedies, comedies, and sonnets, William Shakespeare (1564–1616) probably wrote the romance during the years 1610–1611. Considered to be from the late period in his career, the play was written when he was forty-seven and had already left London and settled in his house at Stratford.

Synonymous with the expression, "an old wives' tale," the title of the play signifies an improbable story, or one in which the very unlikeliness of the melodramatic spectacle is its principal attraction. This fanciful tale was not an original creation by Shakespeare. In fact, the bulk of his work was based on stories initially popularized by other authors during his lifetime. These tales—regarded as contemporary favorites of the time—had the best potential for luring audiences to the theatre. Shakespeare's selection of material for *The Winter's Tale* is no exception; the plot is based on *Pandosto, the Triumph of Time* (1588), a novel by Robert Greene, one of Shakespeare's literary rivals. Analogously, Greene's work was itself conceived from an actual incident that occurred in the Bohemian and Polish courts in the late 14th century. The work was later reprinted and known as *Dorastus and Fawnia* (1607), retitled after the names of the young lovers in the story (Florizel and Perdita in Shakespeare's version).

Remaining generally faithful to the events in the original tale, Shakespeare nonetheless incorporated changes to the plot and added new characters, adapting the material to his own thematic ends. Infusing the story with a perspective uniquely his own, he divides the play into two distinct parts, the first tragic, the second comic. The convincing union of these parts into a harmonious whole represents what many critics have cited as Shakespeare's clearest and most successful example of the tragicomedy.

Contents

Dramatis Personæ[1]

LEONTES, king of Sicilia.
MAMILLIUS, young prince of Sicilia.
CAMILLO,
ANTIGONUS,
CLEOMENES, } Four Lords of Sicilia.
DION,
POLIXENES, king of Bohemia.
FLORIZEL, prince of Bohemia.
ARCHIDAMUS, a Lord of Bohemia.
Old Shepherd, reputed father of Perdita.
Clown, his son.
AUTOLYCUS, a rogue.
A Mariner.
A Gaoler.

HERMIONE, queen to Leontes.
PERDITA, daughter to Leontes and Hermione.
PAULINA, wife to Antigonus.
EMILIA, a lady attending on Hermione.
MOPSA, } Shepherdesses.
DORCAS,

Other Lords and Gentlemen, Ladies, Officers,
and Servants, Shepherds, and Shepherdesses.

Time, as Chorus.

SCENE—*Partly in Sicilia, and partly in Bohemia*

[1]"The Winter's Tale" was printed for the first time in the First Folio of 1623.

ACT I

SCENE I. *Antechamber in Leontes' Palace*

Enter CAMILLO *and* ARCHIDAMUS

ARCHIDAMUS. If you shall chance, Camillo, to visit Bohemia,[1] on the like occasion whereon my services are now on foot, you shall see, as I have said, great difference betwixt our Bohemia and your Sicilia.

CAM. I think, this coming summer, the King of Sicilia means to pay Bohemia the visitation which he justly owes him.

ARCH. Wherein our entertainment shall shame us we will be justified in our loves;[2] for indeed —

CAM. Beseech you, —

ARCH. Verily, I speak it in the freedom of my knowledge: we cannot with such magnificence — in so rare — I know not what to say. We will give you sleepy drinks, that your senses, unintelligent of our insufficience, may, though they cannot praise us, as little accuse us.

CAM. You pay a great deal too dear for what's given freely.

ARCH. Believe me, I speak as my understanding instructs me, and as mine honesty puts it to utterance.

CAM. Sicilia cannot show himself over-kind to Bohemia.[3] They were trained together in their childhoods; and there rooted betwixt them then such an affection, which cannot choose but branch now. Since their more mature dignities and royal necessities made separation of their society, their encounters, though not personal, have been royally attorneyed[4] with interchange of gifts, letters, loving embassies; that they have seemed to be together, though absent; shook hands, as over a vast;[5] and embraced, as it were, from the ends of opposed winds. The heavens continue their loves!

[1]*Bohemia*] the King of Bohemia.
[2]*Wherein . . . loves*] In so far as our entertainment shall discredit us through inefficiency, we will make up the defect with our love.
[3]*Sicilia . . . Bohemia*] The King of Sicilia . . . the King of Bohemia.
[4]*royally attorneyed*] done royally by attorney or deputy.
[5]*vast*] vast sea.

1

ARCH.   I think there is not in the world either malice or matter to alter
    it. You have an unspeakable comfort of your young prince
    Mamillius: it is a gentleman of the greatest promise that ever came
    into my note.

CAM.   I very well agree with you in the hopes of him: it is a gallant
    child; one that indeed physics the subject,[6] makes old hearts fresh:
    they that went on crutches ere he was born desire yet their life to
    see him a man.

ARCH.   Would they else be content to die?

CAM.   Yes; if there were no other excuse why they should desire to
    live.

ARCH.   If the king had no son, they would desire to live on crutches
    till he had one.   [*Exeunt.*

SCENE II. *A Room of State in the Same*

Enter LEONTES, HERMIONE, MAMILLIUS, POLIXENES, CAMILLO, *and*
    Attendants

POL.   Nine changes of the watery star[1] hath been
    The shepherd's note since we have left our throne
    Without a burthen: time as long again
    Would be fill'd up, my brother, with our thanks;
    And yet we should, for perpetuity,
    Go hence in debt: and therefore, like a cipher,
    Yet standing in rich place, I multiply
    With one "We thank you," many thousands moe
    That go before it.

LEON.   Stay your thanks a while;
    And pay them when you part.[2]

POL.   Sir, that's to-morrow.
    I am question'd by my fears, of what may chance
    Or breed upon our absence; that may blow
    No sneaping winds at home, to make us say
    "This is put forth too truly:"[3] besides, I have stay'd

---

[6]*physics the subject*] makes healthy or cheerful the people subject to him, acts as a cordial to the nation.

---

[1]*Nine changes of the watery star*] Nine lunar months. The watery star is the moon,
which governs the tides.

[2]*when you part*] when you depart.

[3]*that may blow . . . truly*] may it be that no nipping winds may blow at home to make
me say "This fear of ill has too good cause."

      To tire your royalty.

LEON.   We are tougher, brother,
      Than you can put us to 't.

POL.   No longer stay.

LEON.   One seven-night longer.

POL.   Very sooth, to-morrow.

LEON.   We'll part the time[4] between 's, then: and in that
      I'll no gainsaying.

POL.   Press me not, beseech you, so.
      There is no tongue that moves, none, none i' the world,
      So soon as yours could win me: so it should now,
      Were there necessity in your request, although
      'T were needful I denied it. My affairs
      Do even drag me homeward: which to hinder
      Were in your love a whip to me; my stay
      To you a charge and trouble: to save both,
      Farewell, our brother.

LEON.   Tongue-tied our queen? speak you.

HER.   I had thought, sir, to have held my peace until
      You had drawn oaths from him not to stay. You, sir,
      Charge him too coldly. Tell him, you are sure
      All in Bohemia's well; this satisfaction
      The by-gone day proclaim'd: say this to him,
      He's beat from his best ward.[5]

LEON.   Well said, Hermione.

HER.   To tell, he longs to see his son, were strong:
      But let him say so then, and let him go;
      But let him swear so, and he shall not stay,
      We'll thwack him hence with distaffs.
      Yet of your royal presence I'll adventure
      The borrow of a week. When at Bohemia
      You take my lord, I'll give him my commission
      To let him there a month behind the gest
      Prefix'd for's parting:[6] yet, good deed,[7] Leontes,
      I love thee not a jar o' the clock[8] behind

---

[4]*part the time*] split the difference as to the time.

[5]*this satisfaction . . . ward*] this satisfactory news was announced yesterday. If you say this
  to him, he is deprived of his best excuse for going.

[6]*let him there . . . parting*] hinder himself or stay there a month beyond the scheduled
  time prearranged for his departure. "Gest," a French word, literally meaning "a lodg-
  ing," was applied to a schedule of lodgings or a time-table of stoppages appointed for
  a royal journey.

[7]*good deed*] indeed.

[8]*a jar o' the clock*] a tick of the clock.

What lady she[9] her lord. You'll stay?

POL.   No, madam.

HER.   Nay, but you will?

POL.   I may not, verily.

HER.   Verily!
> You put me off with limber[10] vows; but I,
> Though you would seek to unsphere the stars[11] with oaths,
> Should yet say "Sir, no going." Verily,
> You shall not go: a lady's "Verily"'s
> As potent as a lord's. Will you go yet?
> Force me to keep you as a prisoner,
> Not like a guest; so you shall pay your fees
> When you depart, and save your thanks. How say you?
> My prisoner? or my guest? by your dread "Verily,"
> One of them you shall be.

POL.   Your guest, then, madam:
> To be your prisoner should import offending;
> Which is for me less easy to commit
> Than you to punish.

HER.   Not your gaoler, then,
> But your kind hostess. Come, I'll question you
> Of my lord's tricks and yours when you were boys:
> You were pretty lordings[12] then?

POL.   We were, fair queen,
> Two lads that thought there was no more behind,
> But such a day to-morrow as to-day,
> And to be boy eternal.

HER.   Was not my lord
> The verier wag o' the two?

POL.   We were as twinn'd lambs that did frisk i' the sun,
> And bleat the one at the other: what we changed[13]
> Was innocence for innocence; we knew not
> The doctrine[14] of ill-doing, nor dream'd
> That any did. Had we pursued that life,
> And our weak spirits ne'er been higher rear'd
> With stronger blood, we should have answer'd heaven

---

[9]*What lady she*] "She" is redundant and adds emphasis to "what lady," *i.e.,* "whatever lady."

[10]*limber*] flexible, untrustworthy, unstable.

[11]*unsphere the stars*] The phrase belongs to the Ptolemaic system of astronomy, which assumed that the stars were each enclosed in a hollow sphere of crystal.

[12]*lordings*] a familiar diminutive of "lords."

[13]*what we changed*] the talk we exchanged.

[14]*doctrine*] here used as a trisyllable.

  Boldly "not guilty;" the imposition clear'd
  Hereditary ours.[15]
HER.   By this we gather
  You have tripp'd since.
POL.   O my most sacred lady!
  Temptations have since then been born to 's: for
  In those unfledged days was my wife a girl;
  Your precious self had then not cross'd the eyes
  Of my young play-fellow.
HER.   Grace to boot![16]
  Of this make no conclusion, lest you say
  Your queen and I are devils: yet go on;
  The offences we have made you do we'll answer,
  If you first sinn'd with us, and that with us
  You did continue fault, and that you slipp'd not
  With any but with us.
LEON.   Is he won yet!
HER. He'll stay, my lord.
LEON.   At my request he would not.
  Hermione, my dearest, thou never spokest
  To better purpose.
HER.   Never?
LEON.   Never, but once.
HER. What! have I twice said well? when was't before?
  I prithee tell me; cram's with praise, and make's
  As fat as tame things: one good deed dying tongueless
  Slaughters a thousand waiting upon that.
  Our praises are our wages: you may ride's
  With one soft kiss a thousand furlongs ere
  With spur we heat an acre.[17] But to the goal:[18]
  My last good deed was to entreat his stay:
  What was my first? it has an elder sister,
  Or I mistake you: O, would her name were Grace!
  But once before I spoke to the purpose: when?
  Nay, let me have 't; I long.
LEON.   Why, that was when
  Three crabbed months had sour'd themselves to death,

---

[15]*the imposition clear'd Hereditary ours*] the imposition or stain of original sin, which
  was ours by heredity, being by our innocence cleared away, altogether removed.
[16]*Grace to boot!*] Pray grace come to our aid!
[17]*heat an acre*] run a heat or course of an acre's length, "acre" being used as a lineal
  measure, equivalent to a furlong.
[18]*to the goal*] to the point.

Ere I could make thee open thy white hand,
And clap[19] thyself my love: then didst thou utter
"I am yours for ever."

HER.   'T is Grace indeed.
Why, lo you now, I have spoke to the purpose twice:
The one for ever earn'd a royal husband;
The other for some while a friend.

To mingle friendship far is mingling bloods.
LEON. [*Aside*]   Too hot, too hot!
I have tremor cordis on me: my heart dances;
But not for joy; not joy. This entertainment
May a free face put on,[20] derive a liberty
From heartiness, from bounty, fertile bosom,[21]
And well become the agent; 't may, I grant;
But to be paddling palms and pinching fingers,
As now they are, and making practised smiles,
As in a looking-glass, and then to sigh, as 't were
The mort o' the deer;[22] O, that is entertainment
My bosom likes not, nor my brows! Mamillius,
Art thou my boy?

MAM.   Ay, my good lord.
LEON.   I' fecks![23]
Why, that's my bawcock.[24] What, hast smutch'd thy nose?
They say it is a copy out of mine. Come, captain,
We must be neat; not neat, but cleanly, captain:
And yet the steer, the heifer and the calf
Are all call'd neat.[25] — Still virginalling[26]
Upon his palm! — How now, you wanton calf!
Art thou my calf?

MAM.   Yes, if you will, my lord.
LEON.   Thou want'st a rough pash and the shoots that I have,[27]

---

[19]*clap*] close the bargain (by clapping hands); acknowledge (thyself my love).

[20]*May a free face put on*] May have an aspect of innocence.

[21]*fertile bosom*] spontaneous exuberance, impulsiveness.

[22]*mort o' the deer*] probably the long-drawn sigh of the dying deer. Although "mort," the French word for death, is technically applied to the musical flourish on the horn which announced in the hunting field the death of the deer, it seems unlikely that Leontes should liken the sighs of secret lovers to the blast of a horn.

[23]*I' fecks*] a colloquial diminutive of "In faith," "I' faith-kins."

[24]*bawcock*] a colloquial term of endearment, from the French "beau coq," "a fine fellow."

[25]*steer . . . heifer . . . calf . . . neat*] horned cattle were generically known as "neat." The allusion is to the horns which were popularly assigned to husbands of faithless wives.

[26]*virginalling*] fingering the musical instrument called the virginal.

[27]*a rough pash . . . have*] a rough head and the horns that shoot from it as I have. The rare word "pash" for "head" seems to be Scottish.

To be full like me: yet they say we are
Almost as like as eggs; women say so,
That will say any thing: but were they false
As o'er-dyed blacks,[28] as wind, as waters, false
As dice are to be wish'd by one that fixes
No bourn[29] 'twixt his and mine, yet were it true
To say this boy were like me. Come, sir page,
Look on me with your welkin eye:[30] sweet villain!
Most dear'st! my collop![31] Can thy dam?[32] — may 't be?—
Affection! thy intention stabs the centre:
Thou dost make possible things not so held,
Communicatest with dreams;—how can this be?—
With what's unreal thou coactive art,
And fellow'st nothing: then 't is very credent
Thou mayst co-join with something; and thou dost,
And that beyond commission, and I find it,
And that to the infection of my brains
And hardening of my brows.[33]

POL.   What means Sicilia?
HER.   He something seems unsettled.
POL.   How, my lord!
What cheer? how is 't with you, best brother?[34]
HER.   You look
As if you held a brow of much distraction:
Are you moved, my lord?
LEON.   No, in good earnest.

---

[28]*o'er-dyed blacks*] stuffs falsely dyed black over their former (light) colour, for purposes
of mourning.

[29]*bourn*] boundary, distinguishing mark. The reference is to one who makes no dis-
tinction between his property and mine, a thief.

[30]*welkin eye*] blue eye, eye of the colour of the welkin or sky.

[31]*my collop*] piece of my flesh.

[32]*Can thy dam?*] Can thy mother (be unchaste)?

[33]*Affection . . . of my brows*] In these abrupt and disjointed sentences Leontes describes
confusedly the disorderly workings of lust ("affection"). The mental connection between the various ejaculations is not easy to define. Some such paraphrase as the following expresses the general meaning; Lust, in its intensity, pierces the very centre or
root of Nature; it makes possible things that are reckoned impossible; it holds com-
munion with dreams; it co-operates with unrealities; it makes companion of nothing-
ness. Yet, moreover, it is quite credible that it should ally itself with actual substance.
Indeed that is just what it does, and does beyond all warrant. I find that mode of lust's
activity now poisoning my brain, and hardening my brows for horns to sprout from.

[34]*How, my lord! . . . brother*] In the Folios this speech is given to Leontes. Hanmer's as-
signment of it to Polixenes seems to improve the context, though Leontes' claim to it
has been defended on the ground that he asks a dissembling counter question by way
of diverting attention from his real state of mind.

How sometimes nature will betray its folly,
Its tenderness, and make itself a pastime
To harder bosoms! Looking on the lines
Of my boy's face, methoughts I did recoil
Twenty-three years, and saw myself unbreech'd,
In my green velvet coat, my dagger muzzled,
Lest it should bite its master, and so prove,
As ornaments oft do, too dangerous:
How like, methought, I then was to this kernel,
This squash,[35] this gentleman. Mine honest friend,
Will you take eggs for money?[36]

MAM.   No, my lord, I'll fight.

LEON.   You will! why, happy man be's dole! My brother,
Are you so fond of your young prince, as we
Do seem to be of ours?

POL.   If at home, sir,
He's all my exercise, my mirth, my matter:
Now my sworn friend, and then mine enemy;
My parasite, my soldier, statesman, all:
He makes a July's day short as December;
And with his varying childness[37] cures in me
Thoughts that would thick my blood.

LEON.   So stands this squire
Officed with me:[38] we two will walk, my lord,
And leave you to your graver steps. Hermione,
How thou lovest us, show in our brother's welcome;
Let what is dear in Sicily be cheap:
Next to thyself and my young rover, he's
Apparent[39] to my heart.

HER.   If you would seek us,
We are yours i' the garden: shall 's attend you there?

LEON.   To your own bents dispose you: you'll be found,
Be you beneath the sky. [*Aside*] I am angling now,
Though you perceive me not how I give line.
Go to, go to!
How she holds up the neb,[40] the bill to him!
And arms her with the boldness of a wife

---

[35]*squash*] unripe peascod.
[36]*take eggs for money*] a proverbial phrase for allowing oneself tamely to be duped.
[37]*childness*] childishness, way of childhood.
[38]*So stands . . . with me*] My young squire fulfils like offices in regard to myself.
[39]*Apparent*] Next-of-kin, as in "heir-apparent."
[40]*neb*] The word usually means a bird's bill or beak. Here it refers to Hermione's mouth.

To her allowing[41] husband!

> [*Exeunt* POLIXENES, HERMIONE, *and* Attendants.

                    Gone already!
Inch-thick, knee-deep, o'er head and ears a fork'd one![42]
Go, play, boy, play: thy mother plays, and I
Play too; but so disgraced a part, whose issue
Will hiss me to my grave: contempt and clamour[43]
Will be my knell. Go, play, boy, play. There have been,
Or I am much deceived, cuckolds ere now;
And many a man there is, even at this present,
Now, while I speak this, holds his wife by the arm,
That little thinks she has been sluiced[44] in 's absence
And his pond fish'd by his next neighbour, by
Sir Smile, his neighbour: nay, there's comfort in 't,
Whiles other men have gates and those gates open'd,
As mine, against their will. Should all despair
That have revolted wives, the tenth of mankind
Would hang themselves. Physic for 't there is none;
It is a bawdy planet, that will strike
Where 't is predominant;[45] and 't is powerful, think it,
From east, west, north and south: be it concluded,
No barricado for a belly; know 't;
It will let in and out the enemy
With bag and baggage: many thousand on 's
Have the disease, and feel 't not. How now, boy!

MAM.   I am like you, they say.
LEON.   Why, that's some comfort.
   What, Camillo there?
CAM.   Ay, my good lord.
LEON.   Go play, Mamillius; thou 'rt an honest man.

> [*Exit* MAMILLIUS.

   Camillo, this great sir will yet stay longer.
CAM.   You had much ado to make his anchor hold:
   When you cast out, it still came home.[46]
LEON.   Didst note it?

---

[41]*allowing*] lawful.
[42]*a fork'd one*] another allusion to the cuckold's brow forked with horns.
[43]*contempt and clamour*] shouts of derision.
[44]*sluiced*] commonly used of drawing off water from, or emptying, a pond.
[45]*It is . . . predominant*] Lust is likened to a planet which, according to astrology, strikes
   or infects all over whose birth it exercises dominating influence.
[46]*it still came home*] the anchor continually refused to hold.

CAM.   He would not stay at your petitions; made
    His business more material.
LEON.   Didst perceive it?
    [*Aside*] They're here with me already; whispering, rounding[47]
    "Sicilia is a so-forth:" 't is far gone,
    When I shall gust it last.[48]—How came 't, Camillo,
    That he did stay?
CAM.   At the good queen's entreaty.
LEON.   At the queen's be 't: "good" should be pertinent;
    But, so it is, it is not. Was this taken[49]
    By any understanding pate but thine?
    For thy conceit is soaking, will draw in
    More than the common blocks:[50] not noted, is 't,
    But of the finer natures? by some severals
    Of head-piece extraordinary?[51] lower messes[52]
    Perchance are to this business purblind?[53] say.
CAM.   Business, my lord! I think most understand
    Bohemia stays here longer.
LEON.   Ha!
CAM.   Stays here longer.
LEON.   Ay, but why?
CAM.   To satisfy your highness, and the entreaties
    Of our most gracious mistress.
LEON.   Satisfy!
    The entreaties of your mistress! satisfy!
    Let that suffice. I have trusted thee, Camillo,
    With all the nearest things to my heart, as well
    My chamber-councils; wherein, priest-like, thou
    Hast cleansed my bosom, I from thee departed
    Thy penitent reform'd: but we have been
    Deceived in thy integrity, deceived
    In that which seems so.
CAM.   Be it forbid, my lord!

---

[47]*They're here . . . rounding*] People already realise my disgrace; they already see the horns on my head; they are whispering, muttering.
[48]*I shall gust it last*] I shall be the last to taste or find it out.
[49]*taken*] apprehended.
[50]*thy conceit . . . blocks*] thy intelligence absorbs or assimilates more than ordinary dull heads.
[51]*by some severals . . . extraordinary*] by some individuals of more than ordinary intellect.
[52]*lower messes*] persons of lower degree, dining at messes set at the lower end of a dining hall.
[53]*purblind*] Here in the original sense of "wholly blind."

LEON.   To bide upon 't,[54] thou art not honest; or,
    If thou inclinest that way, thou art a coward,
    Which hoxes[55] honesty behind, restraining
    From course required; or else thou must be counted
    A servant grafted in my serious trust
    And therein negligent; or else a fool
    That seest a game play'd home, the rich stake drawn,[56]
    And takest it all for jest.
CAM.   My gracious lord,
    I may be negligent, foolish and fearful;
    In every one of these no man is free,
    But that his negligence, his folly, fear,
    Among the infinite doings of the world,
    Sometime puts forth.[57] In your affairs, my lord,
    If ever I were wilful-negligent,
    It was my folly; if industriously[58]
    I play'd the fool, it was my negligence,
    Not weighing well the end; if ever fearful
    To do a thing, where I the issue doubted,
    Whereof the execution did cry out
    Against the non-performance,[59] 't was a fear
    Which oft infects the wisest: these, my lord,
    Are such allow'd infirmities that honesty
    Is never free of. But, beseech your Grace,
    Be plainer with me; let me know my trespass
    By its own visage: if I then deny it,
    'T is none of mine.
LEON.   Ha' not you seen, Camillo,—
    But that 's past doubt, you have, or your eye-glass[60]
    Is thicker than a cuckold's horn,—or heard,—
    For to a vision so apparent rumour
    Cannot be mute,—or thought,—for cogitation
    Resides not in that man that does not think,—
    My wife is slippery? If thou wilt confess,

[54]*To bide upon 't*] To dwell upon this point.
[55]*hoxes*] a variant of the more common "hough" or "hock," "to hamstring," "to cut the sinews."
[56]*a game play'd home . . . drawn*] a game played in all seriousness, the large stake won (by a fellow-player).
[57]*puts forth*] appears, shows up.
[58]*industriously*] on purpose, like the Latin *de industria*.
[59]*Whereof the execution . . . non-performance*] the act, performance of which was so absolutely necessary that the call (to action) forbade neglect.
[60]*eye-glass*] glasslike cover of the eye, the visual organ.

Or else be impudently negative,
To have nor eyes nor ears nor thought, then say
My wife's a hobby-horse;[61] deserves a name
As rank as any flax-wench that puts to
Before her troth-plight: say 't and justify 't.
CAM.   I would not be a stander-by to hear
My sovereign mistress clouded so,[62] without
My present vengeance taken: 'shrew my heart,
You never spoke what did become you less
Than this; which to reiterate were sin[63]
As deep as that, though true.
LEON.   Is whispering nothing?
Is leaning cheek to cheek? is meeting noses?
Kissing with inside lip? stopping the career
Of laughter with a sigh?—a note unfallible
Of breaking honesty;—horsing foot on foot?
Skulking in corners? wishing clocks more swift?
Hours, minutes? noon, midnight? and all eyes
Blind with the pin and web[64] but theirs, theirs only,
That would unseen be wicked? is this nothing?
Why, then the world and all that 's in 't is nothing;
The covering sky is nothing; Bohemia nothing;
My wife is nothing; nor nothing have these nothings,
If this be nothing.
CAM.   Good my lord, be cured
Of this diseased opinion, and betimes;
For 't is most dangerous.
LEON.   Say it be, 't is true.
CAM.   No, no, my lord.
LEON.   It is; you lie, you lie:
I say thou liest, Camillo, and I hate thee,
Pronounce thee a gross lout, a mindless slave,
Or else a hovering temporizer,[65] that
Canst with thine eyes at once see good and evil,
Inclining to them both: were my wife's liver
Infected as her life, she would not live
The running of one glass.
CAM.   Who does infect her?

---

[61]*hobby-horse*] "Hobby-horse" is often applied to a woman of light character.
[62]*clouded so*] blackened so.
[63]*though true*] even granting the accusation of sin were well founded.
[64]*pin and web*] cataract of the eye.
[65]*a hovering temporizer*] a wavering opportunist.

LEON.   Why, he that wears her like her medal, hanging
    About his neck, Bohemia: who, if I
    Had servants true about me, that bare eyes
    To see alike mine honour as their profits,
    Their own particular thrifts, they would do that
    Which should undo more doing: ay, and thou,
    His cupbearer,—whom I from meaner form
    Have bench'd and rear'd to worship, who mayst see
    Plainly as heaven sees earth and earth sees heaven,
    How I am gall'd,—mightst bespice a cup,
    To give mine enemy a lasting wink;
    Which draught to me were cordial.
CAM.   Sir, my lord,
    I could do this, and that with no rash potion,
    But with a lingering dram, that should not work
    Maliciously like poison: but I cannot
    Believe this crack to be in my dread mistress,
    So sovereignly being honourable.[66]
    I have loved thee,—
LEON.   Make that thy question,[67] and go rot!
    Dost think I am so muddy, so unsettled,
    To appoint myself in this vexation;[68] sully
    The purity and whiteness of my sheets,
    Which to preserve is sleep, which being spotted
    Is goads, thorns, nettles, tails of wasps;
    Give scandal to the blood o' the prince my son,
    Who I do think is mine and love as mine,
    Without ripe moving to 't? Would I do this?
    Could man so blench?[69]
CAM.   I must believe you, sir:
    I do; and will fetch off Bohemia[70] for 't;
    Provided that, when he's removed, your highness
    Will take again your queen as yours at first,
    Even for your son's sake; and thereby for sealing
    The injury of tongues[71] in courts and kingdoms
    Known and allied to yours.

[66]*So sovereignly being honourable*] Being so supremely honourable.
[67]*Make that thy question*] Raise doubt about this matter.
[68]*To appoint myself in this vexation*] To make this trouble my business. "Appoint" is frequently found in the sense of "settle" or "arrange," (a matter of business). Hence the modern "appointment," *i.e.*, fixed arrangement.
[69]*Could man so blench*] Could one shrink to such a degree from just behaviour?
[70]*fetch off Bohemia*] make away with, murder, the King of Bohemia.
[71]*sealing . . . tongues*] silencing slanderous tongues.

LEON.   Thou dost advise me
      Even so as I mine own course have set down:
      I'll give no blemish to her honour, none.
CAM.   My lord,
      Go then; and with a countenance as clear
      As friendship wears at feasts, keep with Bohemia
      And with your queen. I am his cupbearer:
      If from me he have wholesome beverage,
      Account me not your servant.
LEON.   This is all:
      Do 't, and thou hast the one half of my heart;
      Do 't not, thou splitt'st thine own.
CAM.   I'll do 't, my lord.
LEON.   I will seem friendly, as thou hast advised me.   [*Exit.*
CAM.   O miserable lady! But, for me,
      What case stand I in? I must be the poisoner
      Of good Polixenes: and my ground to do 't
      Is the obedience to a master, one
      Who, in rebellion with himself, will have
      All that are his so too. To do this deed,
      Promotion follows. If I could find example
      Of thousands that had struck anointed kings
      And flourish'd after, I 'ld not do 't; but since
      Nor brass nor stone nor parchment bears not one,
      Let villany itself forswear 't. I must
      Forsake the court: to do 't, or no, is certain
      To me a break-neck. Happy star reign now!
      Here comes Bohemia.

Re-enter POLIXENES

POL.   This is strange: methinks
      My favour here begins to warp. Not speak?
      Good day, Camillo.
CAM.   Hail, most royal sir!
POL.   What is the news i' the court?
CAM.   None rare, my lord.
POL.   The king hath on him such a countenance
      As he had lost some province, and a region
      Loved as he loves himself: even now I met him
      With customary compliment; when he,
      Wafting his eyes to the contrary, and falling
      A lip of much contempt, speeds from me and
      So leaves me, to consider what is breeding

That changes thus his manners.[72]
CAM.   I dare not know, my lord.
POL.   How! dare not! do not. Do you know, and dare not?
  Be intelligent[73] to me: 't is thereabouts;
  For, to yourself, what you do know, you must,
  And cannot say, you dare not. Good Camillo,
  Your changed complexions are to me a mirror
  Which shows me mine changed too; for I must be
  A party in this alteration, finding
  Myself thus alter'd with 't.
CAM.   There is a sickness
  Which puts some of us in distemper; but
  I cannot name the disease; and it is caught
  Of you that yet are well.
POL.   How! caught of me!
  Make me not sighted like the basilisk:[74]
  I have look'd on thousands, who have sped the better
  By my regard, but kill'd none so. Camillo,—
  As you are certainly a gentleman; thereto
  Clerk-like experienced, which no less adorns
  Our gentry[75] than our parents' noble names,
  In whose success we are gentle,[76]—I beseech you,
  If you know aught which does behove my knowledge
  Thereof to be inform'd, imprison 't not
  In ignorant concealment.
CAM.   I may not answer.
POL.   A sickness caught of me, and yet I well!
  I must be answer'd. Dost thou hear, Camillo?
  I conjure thee, by all the parts of man
  Which honour does acknowledge,[77] whereof the least
  Is not this suit of mine, that thou declare
  What incidency[78] thou dost guess of harm
  Is creeping toward me; how far off, how near;
  Which way to be prevented, if to be;

---

[72]*That changes thus his manners*] Leontes had clearly broken his promise to Camillo to treat Polixenes with every appearance of friendship; his feelings prove too strong for any evasion.
[73]*Be intelligent*] Give intelligence.
[74]*basilisk*] a fabulous serpent, also called "cockatrice," which was said to kill those on whom it fixed its sight.
[75]*gentry*] rank of gentleman.
[76]*In whose . . . gentle*] To succession from whom we owe our gentle blood.
[77]*all the parts . . . acknowledge*] all the duties imposed by honour on man.
[78]*incidency*] contingency or likelihood.

If not, how best to bear it.

CAM. Sir, I will tell you;
Since I am charged in honour and by him
That I think honourable: therefore mark my counsel,
Which must be ev'n as swiftly follow'd as
I mean to utter it, or both yourself and me
Cry lost, and so good night!

POL. On, good Camillo.

CAM. I am appointed him to murder you.[79]

POL. By whom, Camillo?

CAM. By the king.

POL. For what?

CAM. He thinks, nay, with all confidence he swears,
As he had seen 't, or been an instrument
To vice[80] you to 't, that you have touch'd his queen
Forbiddenly.

POL. O then, my best blood turn
To an infected jelly, and my name
Be yoked with his that did betray the Best![81]
Turn then my freshest reputation to
A savour that may strike the dullest nostril
Where I arrive, and my approach be shunn'd,
Nay, hated too, worse than the great'st infection
That e'er was heard or read!

CAM. Swear his thought over[82]
By each particular star in heaven and
By all their influences, you may as well
Forbid the sea for to obey the moon,
As or by oath remove or counsel shake
The fabric of his folly, whose foundation
Is piled upon his faith,[83] and will continue
The standing of his body.

POL. How should this grow?

CAM. I know not: but I am sure 't is safer to
Avoid what's grown than question how 't is born.
If therefore you dare trust my honesty,

---

[79]*him to murder you*] the man to murder you.

[80]*To vice*] To screw.

[81]*his that . . . Best*] Judas Iscariot. Excommunicated persons were formally condemned to "have part with Judas that betrayed Christ."

[82]*Swear his thought over*] Swear his belief down; overcome his opinion by swearing oaths as numerous as the stars.

[83]*piled upon his faith*] set on the basis of his fixed belief.

That lies enclosed in this trunk[84] which you
Shall bear along impawn'd, away to-night!
Your followers I will whisper to the business;
And will by twos and threes at several posterns,
Clear them o' the city. For myself, I'll put
My fortunes to your service, which are here
By this discovery lost. Be not uncertain;
For, by the honour of my parents, I
Have utter'd truth: which if you seek to prove,
I dare not stand by; nor shall you be safer
Than one condemn'd by the king's own mouth, thereon
His execution sworn.

POL.   I do believe thee:
I saw his heart in 's face. Give me thy hand:
Be pilot to me and thy places shall
Still neighbour mine.[85] My ships are ready, and
My people did expect my hence departure
Two days ago. This jealousy
Is for a precious creature: as she's rare,
Must it be great; and, as his person's mighty,
Must it be violent; and as he does conceive
He is dishonour'd by a man which ever
Profess'd[86] to him, why, his revenges must
In that be made more bitter. Fear o'ershades me:
Good expedition be my friend, and comfort
The gracious queen, part of his theme, but nothing
Of his ill-ta'en suspicion![87] Come, Camillo;
I will respect thee as a father if
Thou bear'st my life off hence: let us avoid.

CAM.   It is in mine authority to command
The keys of all the posterns: please your highness
To take the urgent hour. Come, sir, away.   [*Exeunt.*

---

[84]*this trunk*] this body of mine. The quibble is continued in the expression *impawn'd*
(*i.e.*, "in pledge") in the next line.
[85]*thy places shall . . . mine*] thy preferments or offices of honour shall be next to mine.
[86]*Profess'd*] Made honourable professions.
[87]*Good expedition . . . suspicion!*] A safe and quick journey befriend me and comfort the
queen, who is theme of half his thoughts, but is no object for his ill-justified
suspicions.

ACT II

SCENE I. *A Room in Leontes' Palace*

Enter HERMIONE, MAMILLIUS, *and* Ladies

HERMIONE.   Take the boy to you: he so troubles me,
    'T is past enduring.
FIRST LADY.   Come, my gracious lord,
    Shall I be your playfellow?
MAM.   No, I'll none of you.
FIRST LADY.   Why, my sweet lord?
MAM.   You'll kiss me hard, and speak to me as if
    I were a baby still. I love you better.
SEC. LADY.   And why so, my lord?
MAM.   Not for because
    Your brows are blacker; yet black brows, they say,
    Become some women best, so that there be not
    Too much hair there, but in a semicircle,
    Or a half-moon made with a pen.
SEC. LADY.   Who taught you this?
MAM.   I learn'd it out of women's faces. Pray now
    What colour are your eyebrows?
FIRST LADY.   Blue, my lord.
MAM.   Nay, that's a mock: I have seen a lady's nose
    That has been blue, but not her eyebrows.
FIRST LADY.   Hark ye;
    The queen your mother rounds apace: we shall
    Present our services to a fine new prince
    One of these days; and then you 'ld wanton with us,
    If we would have you.
SEC. LADY.   She is spread of late
    Into a goodly bulk: good time encounter her!
HER.   What wisdom stirs amongst you? Come, sir, now
    I am for you again: pray you, sit by us,

And tell 's a tale.

MAM.   Merry or sad shall 't be?

HER.   As merry as you will.

MAM.   A sad tale 's best for winter: I have one
     Of sprites and goblins.

HER.   Let 's have that, good sir.
     Come on, sit down: come on, and do your best
     To fright me with your sprites; you're powerful at it.

MAM.   There was a man—

HER.   Nay, come, sit down; then on.

MAM.   Dwelt by a churchyard: I will tell it softly;
     Yond crickets shall not hear it.

HER.   Come on, then,
     And give 't me in mine ear.

Enter LEONTES, *with* ANTIGONUS, Lords, *and* others

LEON.   Was he met there? his train? Camillo with him?

FIRST LORD.   Behind the tuft of pines I met them; never
     Saw I men scour so on their way: I eyed them
     Even to their ships.

LEON.   How blest am I
     In my just censure, in my true opinion!
     Alack, for lesser knowledge![1] how accursed
     In being so blest! There may be in the cup
     A spider steep'd, and one may drink, depart,
     And yet partake no venom; for his knowledge
     Is not infected: but if one present
     The abhorr'd ingredient to his eye, make known
     How he hath drunk, he cracks his gorge, his sides,
     With violent hefts. I have drunk, and seen the spider.
     Camillo was his help in this, his pandar:
     There is a plot against my life, my crown;
     All 's true that is mistrusted:[2] that false villain
     Whom I employ'd was pre-employ'd by him:
     He has discover'd my design, and I
     Remain a pinch'd thing;[3] yea, a very trick
     For them to play at will. How came the posterns
     So easily open?

FIRST LORD.   By his great authority;
     Which often hath no less prevail'd than so

[1]*Alack, . . . knowledge*] Alas, would that my knowledge were less.
[2]*All's true that is mistrusted*] All that I suspected is true.
[3]*a pinch'd thing*] a shrunk, shrivelled thing, a nonentity.

    On your command.

LEON.   I know 't too well.
    Give me the boy: I am glad you did not nurse him:
    Though he does bear some signs of me, yet you
    Have too much blood in him.

HER.   What is this? sport?

LEON.   Bear the boy hence; he shall not come about her;
    Away with him! and let her sport herself
    With that she 's big with; for 't is Polixenes
    Has made thee swell thus.

HER.   But I 'ld say he had not,
    And I 'll be sworn you would believe my saying,
    Howe'er you learn to the nayward.[4]

LEON.   You, my lords,
    Look on her, mark her well; be but about
    To say "she is a goodly lady," and
    The justice of your hearts will thereto add
    "'T is pity she 's not honest, honourable:"
    Praise her but for this her without-door form,
    Which on my faith deserves high speech, and straight
    The shrug, the hum or ha, these petty brands[5]
    That calumny doth use; O, I am out,
    That mercy does, for calumny will sear
    Virtue itself: these shrugs, these hums and ha's,
    When you have said "she 's goodly," come between
    Ere you can say "she 's honest:" but be 't known,
    From him that has most cause to grieve it should be,
    She 's an adulteress.

HER.   Should a villain say so,
    The most replenish'd villain in the world,
    He were as much more villain: you, my lord,
    Do but mistake.

LEON.   You have mistook, my lady,
    Polixenes for Leontes: O thou thing!
    Which I 'll not call a creature of thy place,[6]
    Lest barbarism, making me the precedent,
    Should a like language use to all degrees,
    And mannerly distinguishment leave out
    Betwixt the prince and beggar: I have said
    She 's an adulteress; I have said with whom:

---

[4]*lean to the nayward*] incline to the denial of it.
[5]*these petty brands*] these little stigmas.
[6]*a creature . . . place*] a person of your rank.

　　　　More, she 's a traitor and Camillo is
　　　　A federary[7] with her; and one that knows,
　　　　What she should shame to know herself
　　　　But with her most vile principal, that she 's
　　　　A bed-swerver, even as bad as those
　　　　That vulgars give bold'st titles; ay, and privy
　　　　To this their late escape.
HER.　　　　　　　　　　　No, by my life,
　　　　Privy to none of this. How will this grieve you,
　　　　When you shall come to clearer knowledge, that
　　　　You thus have publish'd me! Gentle my lord,
　　　　You scarce can right me throughly then to say
　　　　You did mistake.
LEON.　　　　　　　No; if I mistake
　　　　In those foundations which I build upon,
　　　　The centre[8] is not big enough to bear
　　　　A school-boy's top. Away with her, to prison!
　　　　He who shall speak for her is afar off guilty
　　　　But that he speaks.[9]
HER.　　　　　　　There 's some ill planet reigns:
　　　　I must be patient till the heavens look
　　　　With an aspect[10] more favourable. Good my lords,
　　　　I am not prone to weeping, as our sex
　　　　Commonly are; the want of which vain dew
　　　　Perchance shall dry your pities: but I have
　　　　That honourable grief lodged here which burns
　　　　Worse than tears drown: beseech you all, my lords,
　　　　With thoughts so qualified as your charities
　　　　Shall best instruct you, measure me; and so
　　　　The king's will be perform'd!
LEON.　　　　　　　　　Shall I be heard?
HER.　　Who is 't that goes with me? Beseech your highness,
　　　　My women may be with me; for you see
　　　　My plight requires it. Do not weep, good fools;
　　　　There is no cause: when you shall know your mistress
　　　　Has deserved prison, then abound in tears
　　　　As I come out: this action I now go on

---

[7]*federary*] a confederate or accomplice.
[8]*The centre*] The centre of the universe, the earth, according to the old system of astronomy.
[9]*is afar off . . . speaks*] is guilty in a remote degree in the mere fact of his speaking for her.
[10]*aspect*] An astrological term, denoting the appearance of the planets.

Is for my better grace.[11] Adieu, my lord:
I never wish'd to see you sorry; now
I trust I shall. My women, come; you have leave.
LEON.   Go, do our bidding; hence!
                              [*Exit* QUEEN, *guarded; with* Ladies.
FIRST LORD.   Beseech your highness, call the queen again.
ANT.   Be certain what you do, sir, lest your justice
Prove violence; in the which three great ones suffer,
Yourself, your queen, your son.
FIRST LORD.   For her, my lord,
I dare my life lay down and will do 't, sir,
Please you to accept it, that the queen is spotless
I' the eyes of heaven and to you; I mean,
In this which you accuse her.
ANT.   If it prove
She 's otherwise, I 'll keep my stables where
I lodge my wife; I 'll go in couples with her;
Than when I feel and see her no farther trust her;[12]
For every inch of woman in the world,
Ay, every dram of woman's flesh is false,
If she be.
LEON.   Hold your peaces.
FIRST LORD.   Good my lord,—
ANT.   It is for you we speak, not for ourselves:
You are abused,[13] and by some putter-on
That will be damn'd for 't; would I knew the villain,
I would land-damn[14] him. Be she honour-flaw'd,
I have three daughters; the eldest is eleven;
The second and the third, nine, and some five;
If this prove true, they 'll pay for 't: by mine honour,
I 'll geld 'em all; fourteen they shall not see,
To bring false generations: they are co-heirs;

[11]*this action . . . grace*] what I am now about to do or experience is for my good.
[12]*I 'll keep my stables where . . . trust her*] This passage, the interpretation of which has
been much disputed, is probably no more than an emphatic declaration, that if
Hermione be proved unchaste, then the speaker will never allow his wife to be out of
his sight. He will have his eye on her, even when he is engaged in hunting or riding.
His horses shall be stabled wherever she may be dwelling. He and she will go about
like hounds coupled together.
[13]*You are abused, etc.*] You are deceived, and by some instigator or plotter.
[14]*land-damn*] abuse with rancour; damn through the land. The form "landam" is re-
ported to be familiar, in this sense, in the dialect of the Cotswolds and in some parts
of Yorkshire.

And I had rather glib[15] myself than they
Should not produce fair issue.
LEON.　　　　　　　　　　　　Cease; no more.
You smell this business with a sense as cold
As is a dead man's nose: but I do see 't and feel 't,
As you feel doing thus; and see withal
The instruments that feel.[16]
ANT.　　　　　　　　　　　　If it be so,
We need no grave to bury honesty:
There 's not a grain of it the face to sweeten
Of the whole dungy earth.
LEON.　　　　　　　　　　What! lack I credit?
FIRST LORD.　I had rather you did lack than I, my lord,
Upon this ground; and more it would content me
To have her honour true than your suspicion,
Be blamed for 't how you might.
LEON.　　　　　　　　　　　Why, what need we
Commune with you of this, but rather follow
Our forceful instigation?[17] Our prerogative
Calls not your counsels, but our natural goodness
Imparts this; which if you, or stupified
Or seeming so in skill,[18] cannot or will not
Relish a truth like us, inform yourselves
We need no more of your advice: the matter,
The loss, the gain, the ordering on 't, is all
Properly ours.
ANT.　　　　　　And I wish, my liege,
You had only in your silent judgement tried it,
Without more overture.[19]
LEON.　　　　　　　　　　How could that be?
Either thou art most ignorant by age,
Or thou wert born a fool. Camillo's flight,
Added to their familiarity,
Which was as gross as ever touch'd[20] conjecture,
That lack'd sight only, nought for approbation[21]

---

[15]*glib*] geld; another dialect word, common in the north of England in the form "lib."
[16]*As you feel . . . instruments that feel*] Apparently Leontes here grasps Antigonus's hand in his own. The "instruments" are doubtless Antigonus's fingers, which "feel" Leontes' movement.
[17]*forceful instigation*] imperative promptings.
[18]*in skill*] of cunning purpose.
[19]*overture*] open disclosure, publicity.
[20]*touch'd*] stirred or inspired.
[21]*approbation*] positive proof.

But only seeing, all other circumstances
Made up to the deed,—doth push on this proceeding:
Yet, for a greater confirmation,
For in an act of this importance 't were
Most piteous to be wild, I have dispatch'd in post[22]
To sacred Delphos, to Apollo's temple,
Cleomenes and Dion, whom you know
Of stuff'd sufficiency:[23] now from the oracle
They will bring all; whose spiritual counsel had,
Shall stop or spur me.[24] Have I done well?
FIRST LORD.   Well done, my lord.
LEON.   Though I am satisfied and need no more
Than what I know, yet shall the oracle
Give rest to the minds of others, such as he
Whose ignorant credulity will not
Come up to the truth. So have we thought it good
From our free person she should be confined,
Lest that the treachery of the two fled hence[25]
Be left her to perform. Come, follow us;
We are to speak in public; for this business
Will raise us all.[26]
ANT. [*Aside*]   To laughter, as I take it,
If the good truth were known.   [*Exeunt.*

SCENE II. *A Prison*

Enter PAULINA, *a* Gentleman, *and* Attendants

PAUL.   The keeper of the prison, call to him;
Let him have knowledge who I am.   [*Exit* Gent.
                              Good lady,
No court in Europe is too good for thee;
What dost thou then in prison?

Re-enter Gentleman, *with the* Gaoler

                              Now, good sir,
You know me, do you not?

[22]*wild, . . . in post*] rash, impetuous, . . . in great haste.
[23]*stuff'd sufficiency*] ample ability.
[24]*stop or spur me*] withhold me or press me forward.
[25]*the two fled hence*] Polixenes and Camillo, whom Leontes suspects of a plot against
   his life and crown.
[26]*raise us all*] rouse, stir up everybody.

GAOL. For a worthy lady
And one who much I honour.
PAUL. Pray you, then,
Conduct me to the queen.
GAOL. I may not, madam:
To the contrary I have express commandment.
PAUL. Here 's ado,
To lock up honesty and honour from
The access of gentle visitors! Is 't lawful, pray you,
To see her women? any of them? Emilia?
GAOL. So please you, madam,
To put apart these your attendants, I
Shall bring Emilia forth.
PAUL. I pray now, call her.
Withdraw yourselves. [*Exeunt* Gentleman *and* Attendants.
GAOL. And, madam,
I must be present at your conference.
PAUL. Well, be 't so, prithee. [*Exit* Gaoler.
Here 's such ado to make no stain a stain
As passes colouring.[1]

Re-enter Gaoler, *with* EMILIA

Dear gentlewoman,
How fares our gracious lady?
EMIL. As well as one so great and so forlorn
May hold together: on her frights and griefs,
Which never tender lady hath borne greater,
She is something before her time deliver'd.
PAUL. A boy?
EMIL. A daughter; and a goodly babe,
Lusty and like to live: the queen receives
Much comfort in 't; says "My poor prisoner,
I am innocent as you."
PAUL. I dare be sworn:
These dangerous unsafe lunes[2] i' the king, beshrew them!
He must be told on 't, and he shall: the office
Becomes a woman best; I 'll take 't upon me:
If I prove honey-mouth'd, let my tongue blister,
And never to my red-look'd anger be
The trumpet any more. Pray you, Emilia,
Commend my best obedience to the queen:

---

[1]*a stain As passes colouring*] a stain that outdoes all painting.
[2]*lunes*] fits of madness.

If she dares trust me with her little babe,
I 'll show 't the king and undertake to be
Her advocate to the loud'st. We do not know
How he may soften at the sight o' the child:
The silence often of pure innocence
Persuades when speaking fails.

EMIL.   Most worthy madam,
Your honour and your goodness is so evident,
That your free undertaking[3] cannot miss
A thriving issue: there is no lady living
So meet for this great errand. Please your ladyship
To visit the next room, I 'll presently
Acquaint the queen of your most noble offer;
Who but to-day hammer'd of[4] this design,
But durst not tempt a minister of honour,
Lest she should be denied.

PAUL.   Tell her, Emilia,
I 'll use that tongue I have: if wit flow from 't
As boldness from my bosom, let 't not be doubted
I shall do good.

EMIL.   Now be you blest for it!
I 'll to the queen: please you, come something nearer.

GAOL.   Madam, if 't please the queen to send the babe,
I know not what I shall incur to pass it,
Having no warrant.

PAUL.   You need not fear it, sir:
This child was prisoner to the womb, and is
By law and process of great nature thence
Freed and enfranchised; not a party to
The anger of the king, nor guilty of,
If any be, the trespass of the queen.

GAOL.   I do believe it.

PAUL.   Do not you fear: upon mine honour, I
Will stand betwixt you and danger.   [*Exeunt.*

SCENE III. *A Room in Leontes' Palace*

Enter LEONTES, ANTIGONUS, Lords, *and* Servants

LEON.   Nor night nor day no rest: it is but weakness
To bear the matter thus; mere weakness. If

---

[3]*free undertaking*] freely offered undertaking.
[4]*hammer'd of*] considered, forged (in the mind).

The cause were not in being,—part o' the cause,
She the adulteress; for the harlot[1] king
Is quite beyond mine arm, out of the blank
And level[2] of my brain, plot-proof; but she
I can hook to me: say that she were gone,
Given to the fire, a moiety of my rest
Might come to me again. Who 's there?

FIRST SERV.   My lord?

LEON.   How does the boy?

FIRST SERV.   He took good rest to-night;
'T is hoped his sickness is discharged.[3]

LEON.   To see his nobleness!
Conceiving the dishonour of his mother,
He straight declined, droop'd, took it deeply,
Fasten'd and fix'd the shame on 't in himself,
Threw off his spirit, his appetite, his sleep,
And downright languish'd. Leave me solely: go,
See how he fares. [*Exit* SERV.] Fie, fie! no thought of him:[4]
The very thought of my revenges that way
Recoil upon me: in himself too mighty,
And in his parties, his alliance; let him be
Until a time may serve: for present vengeance,
Take it on her. Camillo and Polixenes
Laugh at me, make their pastime at my sorrow:
They should not laugh if I could reach them, nor
Shall she within my power.

Enter PAULINA, *with a child*

FIRST LORD.   You must not enter.

PAUL.   Nay, rather, good my lords, be second to me:
Fear you his tyrannous passion more, alas,
Than the queen's life? a gracious innocent soul,
More free[5] than he is jealous.

ANT.   That 's enough.

SEC. SERV.   Madam, he hath not slept to-night; commanded
None should come at him.

PAUL.   Not so hot, good sir:

---

[1]*harlot*] a term of abuse used of men as well as of women.
[2]*blank And level*] mark and aim; technical terms of archery and gunnery.
[3]*discharged*] dispelled.
[4]*no thought of him*] Leontes by a characteristically abrupt transition here refers to Polixenes.
[5]*More free*] *sc.* from taint.

    I come to bring him sleep. 'T is such as you,
That creep like shadows by him, and do sigh
At each his needless heavings, such as you
Nourish the cause of his awaking: I
Do come with words as medicinal as true,
Honest as either, to purge him of that humour
That presses him from sleep.

LEON.   What noise there, ho?
PAUL.   No noise, my lord; but needful conference
About some gossips[6] for your highness.
LEON.   How!
    Away with that audacious lady! Antigonus,
I charged thee that she should not come about me:
I knew she would.
ANT.   I told her so, my lord,
On your displeasure's peril and on mine,
She should not visit you.
LEON.   What, canst not rule her?
PAUL.   From all dishonesty he can: in this,
Unless he take the course that you have done,
Commit me for committing honour,[7] trust it,
He shall not rule me.
ANT.   La you now, you hear:
When she will take the rein I let her run;
But she 'll not stumble.
PAUL.   Good my liege, I come;
And, I beseech you, hear me, who professes
Myself your loyal servant, your physician,
Your most obedient counsellor, yet that dares
Less appear so in comforting your evils,[8]
Than such as most seem yours: I say, I come
From your good queen.
LEON.   Good queen!
PAUL.   Good queen, my lord,
Good queen; I say good queen;
And would by combat make her good, so were I
A man, the worst about you.
LEON.   Force her hence.

---

[6]*gossips*] sponsors or godparents of the new-born babe.
[7]*Commit . . . honour*] Imprison me for committing an honourable action.
[8]*comforting your evils*] encouraging or abetting your evil courses. The meaning is, that,
  when condonation of the king's offences is in question, Paulina dares appear to be less
  loyal than the men whom Leontes takes to be his best friends.

PAUL.   Let him that makes but trifles of his eyes
    First hand me: on mine own accord I 'll off;
    But first I 'll do my errand. The good queen,
    For she is good, hath brought you forth a daughter;
    Here 't is; commends it to your blessing.
                        [*Laying down the child.*

LEON.   Out!
    A mankind[9] witch! Hence with her, out o' door:
    A most intelligencing[10] bawd!

PAUL.   Not so:
    I am as ignorant in that as you
    In so entitling me, and no less honest
    Than you are mad; which is enough, I 'll warrant,
    As this world goes, to pass for honest.

LEON.   Traitors!
    Will you not push her out? Give her the bastard.
    Thou dotard! thou art woman-tired,[11] unroosted
    By thy dame Partlet[12] here. Take up the bastard;
    Take 't up, I say; give 't to thy crone.

PAUL.   For ever
    Unvenerable be thy hands, if thou
    Takest up the princess by that forced baseness[13]
    Which he has put upon 't!

LEON.   He dreads his wife.

PAUL.   So I would you did; then 't were past all doubt
    You 'ld call your children yours.

LEON.   A nest of traitors!

ANT.   I am none, by this good light.[14]

PAUL.   Nor I; nor any
    But one that 's here, and that 's himself; for he
    The sacred honour of himself, his queen's,
    His hopeful son's, his babe's, betrays to slander,
    Whose sting is sharper than the sword's; and will not,—
    For, as the case now stands, it is a curse
    He cannot be compell'd to 't,—once remove
    The root of his opinion, which is rotten

---

[9]*mankind*] virago or termagant, used adjectivally.

[10]*intelligencing*] acting as go-between.

[11]*woman-tired*] henpecked. In falconry "to tire" is to "peck" or tear with the beak.

[12]*dame Partlet*] a colloquial name for a hen; apparently first so applied in the popular
story of "Reynard the Fox."

[13]*by that forced baseness*] under that false appellation of bastardy, which Leontes has
just uttered.

[14]*by this good light*] in this full light of day.

As ever oak or stone was sound.

LEON.   A callat[15]
Of boundless tongue, who late hath beat her husband
And now baits me! This brat is none of mine;
It is the issue of Polixenes:
Hence with it, and together with the dam
Commit them to the fire!

PAUL.   It is yours;
And, might we lay the old proverb[16] to your charge,
So like you, 't is the worse. Behold, my lords,
Although the print be little, the whole matter
And copy of the father, eye, nose, lip;
The thick of 's frown; his forehead; nay, the valley,
The pretty dimples of his chin and cheek; his smiles;
The very mould and frame of hand, nail, finger:
And thou, good goddess Nature, which hast made it
So like to him that got it, if thou hast
The ordering of the mind too, 'mongst all colours
No yellow[17] in 't, lest she suspect, as he does,
Her children not her husband's!

LEON.   A gross hag!
And, lozel, thou art worthy to be hang'd,
That wilt not stay her tongue.

ANT.   Hang all the husbands
That cannot do that feat, you 'll leave yourself
Hardly one subject.

LEON.   Once more, take her hence.

PAUL.   A most unworthy and unnatural lord
Can do no more.

LEON.   I 'll ha' thee burnt.

PAUL.   I care not:
It is an heretic that makes the fire,
Not she which burns in 't. I 'll not call you tyrant;
But this most cruel usage of your queen—
Not able to produce more accusation
Than your own weak-hinged fancy—something savours
Of tyranny, and will ignoble make you,
Yea, scandalous to the world.

LEON.   On your allegiance,

---

[15]*callat*] a woman of bad character.
[16]*the old proverb*] "The better the worser" (of a good deed productive of evil
  consequences).
[17]*yellow*] the colour of jealousy.

Out of the chamber with her! Were I a tyrant,
Where were her life? she durst not call me so,
If she did know me one. Away with her!
PAUL. I pray you, do not push me; I 'll be gone.
Look to your babe, my lord; 't is yours: Jove send her
A better guiding spirit! What needs these hands?
You, that are thus so tender o'er his follies,
Will never do him good, not one of you.
So, so: farewell; we are gone. [*Exit.*
LEON. Thou, traitor, hast set on thy wife to this.
My child? away with 't! Even thou, that hast
A heart so tender o'er it, take it hence
And see it instantly consumed with fire;
Even thou and none but thou. Take it up straight:
Within this hour bring me word 't is done,
And by good testimony, or I 'll seize thy life,
With what thou else call'st thine. If thou refuse
And wilt encounter with my wrath, say so;
The bastard brains with these my proper hands
Shall I dash out. Go, take it to the fire;
For thou set'st on thy wife.
ANT.   I did not, sir:
These lords, my noble fellows,[18] if they please,
Can clear me in 't.
LORDS.   We can: my royal liege,
He is not guilty of her coming hither.
LEON. You 're liars all.
FIRST LORD. Beseech your highness, give us better credit:
We have always truly served you; and beseech you
So to esteem of us: and on our knees we beg,
As recompense of our dear[19] services
Past and to come, that you do change this purpose,
Which being so horrible, so bloody, must
Lead on to some foul issue: we all kneel.
LEON. I am a feather for each wind that blows:
Shall I live on to see this bastard kneel
And call me father? better burn it now
Than curse it then. But be it; let it live.
It shall not neither. You, sir, come you hither;
You that have been so tenderly officious
With Lady Margery, your midwife there,

[18]*fellows*] colleagues.
[19]*dear*] devoted.

To save this bastard's life,—for 't is a bastard,
So sure as this beard's[20] grey,—what will you adventure
To save this brat's life?

ANT.   Any thing, my lord,
That my ability may undergo,
And nobleness impose: at least thus much:
I 'll pawn the little blood which I have left
To save the innocent: any thing possible.

LEON.   It shall be possible. Swear by this sword
Thou wilt perform my bidding.

ANT.   I will, my lord.

LEON.   Mark and perform it: seest thou? for the fail
Of any point in 't shall not only be
Death to thyself but to thy lewd-tongued wife,
Whom for this time we pardon. We enjoin thee,
As thou art liege-man to us, that thou carry
This female bastard hence, and that thou bear it
To some remote and desert place, quite out
Of our dominions; and that there thou leave it,
Without more mercy, to its own protection
And favour of the climate. As by strange fortune
It came to us, I do in justice charge thee,
On thy soul's peril and thy body's torture,
That thou commend it strangely[21] to some place
Where chance may nurse or end it. Take it up.

ANT.   I swear to do this, though a present death
Had been more merciful. Come on, poor babe:
Some powerful spirit instruct the kites and ravens
To be thy nurses! Wolves and bears, they say,
Casting their savageness aside have done
Like offices of pity. Sir, be prosperous
In more than this deed does require! And blessing
Against this cruelty fight on thy side,
Poor thing, condemn'd to loss![22]   [*Exit with the child.*

LEON.   No, I 'll not rear
Another's issue.

---

[20]*this beard's*] This is the Folio reading, which has been variously changed to *his* and *thy*. The reference is clearly to Antigonus's beard, at which Leontes may be supposed to point his finger.

[21]*commend it strangely*] commit it as a stranger. "Commended" is similarly used for "committed."

[22]*condemn'd to loss*] In Baret's *Alvearie*, 1580, "loss" is defined "'hurt,' properly things cast out of a shippe in time of a tempest."

Enter a Servant

SERV.   Please your highness, posts
    From those you sent to the oracle are come
    An hour since: Cleomenes and Dion,
    Being well arrived from Delphos, are both landed,
    Hasting to the court.
FIRST LORD.   So please you, sir, their speed
    Hath been beyond account.
LEON.   Twenty three days
    They have been absent: 't is good speed; foretells
    The great Apollo suddenly will have
    The truth of this appear. Prepare you, lords;
    Summon a session, that we may arraign
    Our most disloyal lady; for, as she hath
    Been publicly accused, so shall she have
    A just and open trial. While she lives
    My heart will be a burthen to me. Leave me,
    And think upon my bidding.   [*Exeunt.*

ACT III

SCENE I. *A Sea-Port in Sicilia*

Enter CLEOMENES *and* DION

CLEOMENES.   The climate's delicate, the air most sweet,
Fertile the isle,[1] the temple much surpassing
The common praise it bears.
DION.   I shall report,
For most it caught me, the celestial habits,
Methinks I so should term them, and the reverence
Of the grave wearers. O, the sacrifice!
How ceremonious, solemn and unearthly
It was i' the offering!
CLEO.   But of all, the burst
And the ear-deafening voice o' the oracle,
Kin to Jove's thunder, so surprised my sense,
That I was nothing.
DION.   If the event o' the journey
Prove as successful to the queen,—O be 't so!—
As it hath been to us rare, pleasant, speedy,
The time is worth the use on 't.
CLEO.   Great Apollo
Turn all to the best! These proclamations,
So forcing faults upon Hermione,
I little like.
DION.   The violent carriage of it
Will clear or end the business: when the oracle,
Thus by Apollo's great divine seal'd up,
Shall the contents discover, something rare

---

[1]*the isle*] Apollo's oracle was at Delphi in Phocis, on the mainland of Greece. But Greene in his novel of *Pandosto*, on which Shakespeare based his play, carelessly located it in the isle of Delphos, and Shakespeare adopted the error.

Even then will rush to knowledge. Go: fresh horses!
And gracious be the issue!   [*Exeunt.*

SCENE II. A *Court of Justice*

Enter LEONTES, Lords, *and* Officers

LEON.   This sessions, to our great grief we pronounce,
    Even pushes 'gainst our heart: the party tried
    The daughter of a king, our wife, and one
    Of us too much beloved. Let us be clear'd
    Of being tyrannous, since we so openly
    Proceed in justice, which shall have due course,
    Even to the guilt or the purgation.[2]
    Produce the prisoner.
OFF.   It is his highness' pleasure that the queen
    Appear in person here in court. Silence![3]

Enter HERMIONE *guarded*; PAULINA *and* Ladies *attending*

LEON.   Read the indictment.
OFF. [*reads*]   Hermione, queen to the worthy Leontes, king of Sicilia, thou
art here accused and arraigned of high treason, in committing adultery
with Polixenes, king of Bohemia, and conspiring with Camillo to take
away the life of our sovereign lord the king, thy royal husband: the pre-
tence whereof being by circumstances partly laid open, thou, Hermione,
contrary to the faith and allegiance of a true subject, didst counsel and
aid them, for their better safety, to fly away by night.
HER.   Since what I am to say must be but that
    Which contradicts my accusation, and
    The testimony on my part no other
    But what comes from myself, it shall scare boot me
    To say "not guilty:" mine integrity,
    Being counted falsehood, shall, as I express it,
    Be so received. But thus, if powers divine
    Behold our human actions, as they do,
    I doubt not then but innocence shall make
    False accusation blush, and tyranny
    Tremble at patience. You, my lord, best know,.
    Who least will seem to do so, my past life
    Hath been as continent, as chaste, as true,

[2]*Even to the guilt or the purgation*] Whether it lead to conviction or acquittal.
[3]*Silence!*] In the Folios this is printed in italics, like a stage direction. But it would seem
  to be the fitting exclamation of the officer of the court.

As I am now unhappy; which is more
Than history can pattern, though devised
And play'd to take spectators. For behold me
A fellow of the royal bed, which owe
A moiety[4] of the throne, a great king's daughter,
The mother to a hopeful prince, here standing
To prate and talk for life and honour 'fore
Who please to come and hear. For life, I prize it
As I weigh grief, which I would spare:[5] for honour,
'T is a derivative from me to mine,
And only that I stand for. I appeal
To your own conscience, sir, before Polixenes
Came to your court, how I was in your grace,
How merited to be so; since he came,
With what encounter so uncurrent I
Have strain'd, to appear thus:[6] if one jot beyond
The bound of honour, or in act or will
That way inclining, harden'd be the hearts
Of all that hear me, and my near'st of kin
Cry fie upon my grave!
LEON.   I ne'er heard yet
That any of these bolder vices wanted
Less impudence to gainsay what they did
Than to perform it first.[7]
HER.   That 's true enough;
Though 't is a saying, sir, not due to me.
LEON.   You will not own it.
HER.   More than mistress of
Which comes to me in name of fault, I must not
At all acknowledge.[8] For Polixenes,
With whom I am accused, I do confess
I loved him as in honour he required,
With such a kind of love as might become
A lady like me, with a love even such,

---

[4]owe A moiety] own a share.
[5]which I would spare] which I would willingly be rid of.
[6]With what . . . thus] With what unwarrantable familiarity of intercourse have I so exceeded bounds as to be condemned to figure as defendant in this kind of suit.
[7]I ne'er . . . first] Cf. Greene's "Novel": "As for her, it was her parte to deny such a monstrous crime, and to be impudent in forswearing the fact, since shee had passed all shame in committing the fault."
[8]More than mistress of . . . acknowledge] It is not for me in any way to admit more knowledge of the grounds of the imputation made against me than I learn from the terms of the charge.

So and no other, as yourself commanded:
Which not to have done I think had been in me
Both disobedience and ingratitude
To you and toward your friend; whose love had spoke,
Even since it could speak, from an infant, freely
That it was yours. Now, for conspiracy,
I know not how it tastes; though it be dish'd
For me to try how: all I know of it
Is that Camillo was an honest man;
And why he left your court, the gods themselves,
Wotting no more than I, are ignorant.

LEON.   You knew of his departure, as you know
What you have underta'en to do in 's absence.

HER.   Sir,
You speak a language that I understand not:
My life stands in the level of[9] your dreams,
Which I 'll lay down.

LEON.   Your actions are my dreams;
You had a bastard by Polixenes,
And I but dream'd it. As you were past all shame,—
Those of your fact[10] are so,—so past all truth:
Which to deny concerns more than avails;[11] for as
Thy brat hath been cast out, like to itself,
No father owning it,—which is, indeed,
More criminal in thee than it,—so thou
Shalt feel our justice, in whose easiest passage[12]
Look for no less than death.

HER.   Sir, spare your threats:
The bug[13] which you would fright me with I seek.
To me can life be no commodity:[14]
The crown and comfort of my life, your favour,
I do give lost; for I do feel it gone,
But know not how it went. My second joy
And first-fruits of my body, from his presence
I am barr'd, like one infectious. My third comfort,
Starr'd most unluckily, is from my breast,

[9]*in the level of*] within the range of, at the mercy of.

[10]*Those of your fact*] See footnote 7 for a quotation from Greene's "Novel," where "fact" is used in the present sense of "criminal action."

[11]*Which to deny . . . avails*] The denial of which has mere academic interest, and lacks practical weight.

[12]*easiest passage*] mildest sentence.

[13]*bug*] bugbear.

[14]*commodity*] profit, advantage.

The innocent milk in it most innocent mouth,
Haled out to murder: myself on every post
Proclaim'd a strumpet: with immodest hatred
The child-bed privilege denied, which 'longs
To women of all fashion; lastly, hurried
Here to this place, i' the open air, before
I have got strength of limit.[15] Now, my liege,
Tell me what blessings I have here alive,
That I should fear to die? Therefore proceed.
But yet hear this; mistake me not; no life,
I prize it not a straw, but for mine honour,
Which I would free, if I shall be condemn'd
Upon surmises, all proofs sleeping else
But what your jealousies awake, I tell you
'T is rigour and not law. Your honours all,
I do refer me to the oracle:
Apollo be my judge!
FIRST LORD.   This your request
    Is altogether just: therefore bring forth,
    And in Apollo's name, his oracle.   [*Exeunt certain* Officers.
HER.   The Emperor of Russia was my father:
    O that he were alive, and here beholding
    His daughter's trial! that he did but see
    The flatness[16] of my misery, yet with eyes
    Of pity, not revenge!

Re-enter Officers, *with* CLEOMENES *and* DION

OFF.   You here shall swear upon this sword of justice,
    That you, Cleomenes and Dion, have
    Been both at Delphos, and from thence have brought
    This seal'd-up oracle, by the hand deliver'd
    Of great Apollo's priest, and that since then
    You have not dared to break the holy seal
    Nor read the secrets in 't.
CLEO. DION.   All this we swear.
LEON.   Break up the seals and read.
OFF. [*reads*]   Hermione is chaste; Polixenes blameless; Camillo a true sub-
    ject; Leontes a jealous tyrant; his innocent babe truly begotten; and the
    king shall live without an heir, if that which is lost be not found.
LORDS.   Now blessed be the great Apollo!

---

[15]*strength of limit*] strength to go to such a limit, so far.
[16]*flatness*] completeness. "Flat" is still similarly used in such phrases as "a flat [*i.e.*, downright] lie."

HER.   Praised!

LEON.   Hast thou read truth?

OFF.   Ay, my lord; even so

    As it is here set down.

LEON.   There is no truth at all i' the oracle:

    The sessions shall proceed: this is mere falsehood.

Enter Servant

SERV.   My lord the king, the king!

LEON.   What is the business?

SERV.   O sir, I shall be hated to report it!

    The prince your son, with mere conceit and fear

    Of the queen's speed,[17] is gone.

LEON.   How! gone!

SERV.   Is dead.

LEON.   Apollo 's angry; and the heavens themselves

    Do strike at my injustice. [HERMIONE *faints.*] How now there!

PAUL.   This news is mortal to the queen: look down

    And see what death is doing.

LEON.   Take her hence:

    Her heart is but o'ercharged; she will recover:

    I have too much believed mine own suspicion:

    Beseech you, tenderly apply to her

    Some remedies for life.

                  [*Exeunt* PAULINA *and ladies, with* HERMIONE.

               Apollo, pardon

    My great profaneness 'gainst thine oracle!

    I 'll reconcile me to Polixenes;

    New woo my queen; recall the good Camillo,

    Whom I proclaim a man of truth, of mercy;

    For, being transported by my jealousies

    To bloody thoughts and to revenge, I chose

    Camillo for the minister to poison

    My friend Polixenes: which had been done,

    But that the good mind of Camillo tardied[18]

    My swift command, though I with death and with

    Reward did threaten and encourage him,

    Not doing it and being done: he, most humane

---

[17]*mere conceit . . . speed*] mere apprehension and fear of the queen's fortune. "Conceit" is applied by Shakespeare to all manner of mental conceptions. With "speed" cf. the modern use of "sped" (*i.e.,* fared).

[18]*tardied*] delayed to execute.

And fill'd with honour, to my kingly guest
Unclasp'd my practice, quit his fortunes here,
Which you knew great, and to the hazard
Of all incertainties himself commended,[19]
No richer than[20] his honour: how he glisters
Thorough my rust! and how his piety
Does my deeds make the blacker!

Re-enter PAULINA

PAUL.   Woe the while!
O, cut my lace, lest my heart, cracking it,
Break too!
FIRST LORD.   What fit is this, good lady?
PAUL.   What studied torments, tyrant, hast for me?
What wheels? racks? fires? what flaying? boiling?[21]
In leads or oils? what old or newer torture
Must I receive, whose every word deserves
To taste of thy most worst? Thy tyranny
Together working with thy jealousies,
Fancies too weak for boys, too green and idle
For girls of nine, O, think what they have done
And then run mad indeed, stark mad! for all
Thy by-gone fooleries were but spices of it.
That thou betray'dst Polixenes, 't was nothing;
That did but show thee, of a fool, inconstant[22]
And damnable ingrateful: nor was 't much,
Thou wouldst have poison'd good Camillo's honour,
To have him kill a king; poor trespasses,
More monstrous standing by: whereof I reckon
The casting forth to crows thy baby-daughter
To be or none or little; though a devil
Would have shed water out of fire[23] ere done 't:
Nor is 't directly laid to thee, the death
Of the young prince, whose honourable thoughts,
Thoughts high for one so tender, cleft the heart
That could conceive a gross and foolish sire
Blemish'd his gracious dam: this is not, no,

---

[19]*commended*] committed.
[20]*No richer than*] With no riches other than.
[21]*boiling?*] Thus the First Folio. The Second and later Folios add *burning* after *boiling* for the sake of metre.
[22]*of a fool, inconstant*] Thus the Folios; there is no need for any change. The meaning is that Leontes, being a fool, shows himself inconstant in addition.
[23]*shed water out of fire*] shed tears amid the flames (of hell).

Laid to thy answer: but the last,—O lords,
When I have said, cry "woe!"—the queen, the queen,
The sweet'st, dear'st creature 's dead, and vengeance for 't
Not dropp'd down yet.
FIRST LORD.   The higher powers forbid!
PAUL.   I say she 's dead, I 'll swear 't. If word nor oath
Prevail not, go and see: if you can bring
Tincture or lustre in her lip, her eye,
Heat outwardly or breath within, I 'll serve you
As I would do the gods. But, O thou tyrant!
Do not repent these things, for they are heavier
Than all thy woes can stir:[24] therefore betake thee
To nothing but despair. A thousand knees
Ten thousand years together, naked, fasting,
Upon a barren mountain, and still winter
In storm perpetual, could not move the gods
To look that way thou wert.
LEON.   Go on, go on:
Thou canst not speak too much; I have deserved
All tongues to talk their bitterest.
FIRST LORD.   Say no more:
Howe'er the business goes, you have made fault
I' the boldness of your speech.
PAUL.   I am sorry for 't:
All faults I make, when I shall come to know them,
I do repent. Alas! I have show'd too much
The rashness of a woman: he is touch'd
To the noble heart. What 's gone and what 's past help
Should be past grief: do not receive affliction
At my petition;[25] I beseech you, rather
Let me be punish'd, that have minded you
Of what you should forget. Now, good my liege,
Sir, royal sir, forgive a foolish woman:
The love I bore your queen, lo, fool again!
I 'll speak of her no more, nor of your children;
I 'll not remember you of my own lord,
Who is lost too: take your patience to you,
And I 'll say nothing.
LEON.   Thou didst speak but well
When most the truth; which I receive much better

---

[24]*woes can stir*] woes self-inflicted by way of penance can remove.
[25]*do not . . . petition*] Thus the Folios. The meaning apparently is: do not accept or give
way to the affliction or sorrow caused by my entreaty or appeal to you.

Than to be pitied of thee. Prithee, bring me
To the dead bodies of my queen and son:
One grave shall be for both; upon them shall
The causes of their death appear, unto
Our shame perpetual. Once a day I 'll visit
The chapel where they lie, and tears shed there
Shall be my recreation: so long as nature
Will bear up with this exercise, so long
I daily vow to use it. Come and lead me
To these sorrows.   [*Exeunt.*

SCENE III. *Bohemia—A Desert Country Near the Sea*

Enter ANTIGONUS *with a* Child, *and a* Mariner

ANT.   Thou art perfect,[1] then, our ship hath touch'd upon
    The deserts of Bohemia?[2]
MAR.   Ay, my lord; and fear
    We have landed in ill time: the skies look grimly
    And threaten present blusters. In my conscience,
    The heavens with that we have in hand are angry
    And frown upon 's.
ANT.   Their sacred wills be done! Go, get aboard;
    Look to thy bark: I 'll not be long before
    I call upon thee.
MAR.   Make your best haste, and go not
    Too far i' the land: 't is like to be loud weather;
    Besides, this place is famous for the creatures
    Of prey that keep upon 't.
ANT.   Go thou away:
    I 'll follow instantly.
MAR.   I am glad at heart
    To be so rid o' the business.   [*Exit.*
ANT.   Come, poor babe:
    I have heard, but not believed, the spirits o' the dead
    May walk again: if such thing be, thy mother

---

[1]*perfect*] certain.
[2]*ship . . . Bohemia*] Ben Jonson adversely criticised Shakespeare for giving Bohemia a
sea-coast. See his *Conversations with Drummond*, 1619, ch. xii. Shakespeare here pre-
cisely follows the like episode in Green's "Novel." It would appear that during the thir-
teenth century the kingdom of Bohemia included provinces on the coast of the
Adriatic. But doubtless Greene was ignorant of such a fact, and committed a geo-
graphical blunder which Shakespeare did not detect.

Appear'd to me last night, for ne'er was dream
So like a waking. To me comes a creature,
Sometimes her head on one side, some another;
I never saw a vessel of like sorrow,
So fill'd and so becoming: in pure white robes,
Like very sanctity, she did approach
My cabin where I lay; thrice bow'd before me,
And, gasping to begin some speech, her eyes
Became two spouts: the fury spent, anon
Did this break from her: "Good Antigonus,
Since fate, against thy better disposition,
Hath made thy person for the thrower-out
Of my poor babe, according to thine oath,
Places remote enough are in Bohemia,
There weep and leave it crying; and, for the babe
Is counted lost for ever, Perdita,
I prithee, call 't. For this ungentle business,
Put on thee by my lord, thou ne'er shalt see
Thy wife Paulina more." And so, with shrieks,
She melted into air. Affrighted much,
I did in time collect myself, and thought
This was so, and no slumber. Dreams are toys:
Yet for this once, yea, superstitiously,
I will be squared by this.[3] I do believe
Hermione hath suffer'd death; and that
Apollo would, this being indeed the issue
Of King Polixenes, it should here be laid,
Either for life or death, upon the earth
Of its right father. Blossom, speed thee well!
There lie, and there thy character:[4] there these;
Which may, if fortune please, both breed thee, pretty,
And still rest thine. The storm begins: poor wretch,
That for thy mother's fault art thus exposed
To loss[5] and what may follow! Weep I cannot,
But my heart bleeds; and most accursed am I
To be by oath enjoin'd to this. Farewell!
The day frowns more and more: thou 'rt like to have
A lullaby too rough: I never saw
The heavens so dim by day. A savage clamour!
Well may I get aboard! This is the chase:

---

[3]*I will be squared by this*] I will be ruled, regulate my conduct, by this vision.
[4]*thy character*] written description of thee.
[5]*loss*] hurt.

I am gone for ever.   [*Exit, pursued by a bear.*

Enter a Shepherd

SHEP.   I would there were no age between ten and three-and-twenty,
   or that youth would sleep out the rest; for there is nothing in
   the between but getting wenches with child, wronging the ancientry,[6] stealing, fighting—Hark you now! Would any but these
   boiled brains[7] of nineteen and two-and-twenty hunt this weather?
   They have scared away two of my best sheep, which I fear the wolf
   will sooner find than the master: if any where I have them, 't is by
   the sea-side, browzing of ivy. Good luck, an 't be thy will! what
   have we here? Mercy on 's, a barne; a very pretty barne![8] A boy or
   a child,[9] I wonder? A pretty one; a very pretty one: sure, some
   scape:[10] though I am not bookish, yet I can read waiting-gentle-
   woman in the scape. This has been some stair-work, some trunk-
   work, some behind-door-work: they were warmer that got this than
   the poor thing is here. I 'll take it up for pity: yet I 'll tarry till my
   son come; he hallooed but even now. Whoa, ho, hoa!

[*Enter* Clown]

CLO.   Hilloa, loa!
SHEP.   What, art so near? If thou 'lt see a thing to talk on when thou
   art dead and rotten, come hither. What ailest thou, man?
CLO.   I have seen two such sights, by sea and by land! but I am not to
   say it is a sea, for it is now the sky: betwixt the firmament and it
   you cannot thrust a bodkin's point.
SHEP.   Why, boy, how is it?
CLO. .   I would you did but see how it chafes, how it rages, how it takes
   up[11] the shore! but that 's not to the point. O, the most piteous cry
   of the poor souls! sometimes to see 'em, and not to see 'em; now
   the ship boring the moon with her main-mast, and anon swallowed with yest and froth, as you 'ld thrust a cork into a hogshead.
   And then for the land-service, to see how the bear tore out his
   shoulder-bone; how he cried to me for help and said his name was
   Antigonus, a nobleman. But to make an end of the ship, to see
   how the sea flap-dragoned[12] it: but, first, how the poor souls

[6]*wronging the ancientry*] wronging their elders.
[7]*boiled brains*] madcaps.
[8]*barne*] a north-country form of "bairn," child.
[9]*child*] This word was often exclusively applied to a baby girl, and is still so employed
   in English provincial dialects.
[10]*scape*] (fruit of) transgression.
[11]*takes up*] rails against.
[12]*flap-dragoned*] swallowed.

roared, and the sea mocked them; and how the poor gentleman
roared and the bear mocked him, both roaring louder than the sea
or weather.

SHEP.   Name of mercy, when was this, boy?

CLO.   Now, now: I have not winked since I saw these sights: the men
are not yet cold under water, nor the bear half dined on the gentleman: he 's at it now.

SHEP.   Would I had been by, to have helped the old man!

CLO.   I would you had been by the ship side, to have helped her:
there your charity would have lacked footing.

SHEP.   Heavy matters! heavy matters! but look thee here, boy. Now
bless thyself: thou mettest with things dying, I with things new-
born. Here 's a sight for thee; look thee, a bearing-cloth[13] for a
squire's child! look thee here; take up, take up, boy; open 't. So,
let 's see: it was told me I should be rich by the fairies. This is some
changeling:[14] open 't. What 's within, boy?

CLO.   You 're a made[15] old man: if the sins of your youth are forgiven
you, you 're well to live. Gold! all gold!

SHEP.   This is fairy gold, boy, and 't will prove so: up with 't, keep it
close: home, home, the next way. We are lucky, boy; and to be so
still requires nothing but secrecy. Let my sheep go: come, good
boy, the next way home.

CLO.   Go you the next way with your findings. I 'll go see if the bear
be gone from the gentleman and how much he hath eaten: they
are never curst[16] but when they are hungry: if there be any of him
left, I 'll bury it.

SHEP.   That 's a good deed. If thou mayest discern by that which is left
of him what he is, fetch me to the sight of him.

CLO.   Marry, will I; and you shall help to put him i' the ground.

SHEP.   'T is a lucky day, boy, and we 'll do good deeds on 't.

                                                    [*Exeunt.*

---

[13]*a bearing-cloth*] a christening mantle.

[14]*changeling*] a child stolen from its parents by the fairies, who are usually credited with
leaving another in its place. The word is more commonly applied to the child alleged
to be substituted by the fairies for the stolen infant.

[15]*made*] Theobald's correction of *mad*, the impossible reading of the Folios. The word
"made" in the present sense figures in like context in Greene's "Novel."

[16]*curst*] ill-tempered, angry.

ACT IV

SCENE I

Enter TIME, *the* Chorus

TIME.   I that please some, try all, both joy and terror
    Of good and bad, that makes and unfolds error,
    Now take upon me, in the name of Time,
    To use my wings. Impute it not a crime
    To me or my swift passage, that I slide
    O'er sixteen years and leave the growth untried
    Of that wide gap,[1] since it is in my power
    To o'erthrow law and in one self-born hour[2]
    To plant and o'erwhelm custom. Let me pass ˙
    The same I am, ere ancient'st order was
    Or what is now received: I witness to
    The times that brought them in; so shall I do
    To the freshest things now reigning, and make stale
    The glistering of this present, as my tale
    Now seems to it.[3] Your patience this allowing,
    I turn my glass and give my scene such growing
    As you had slept between: Leontes leaving,
    The effects of his fond jealousies so grieving
    That he shuts up himself, imagine me,[4]
    Gentle spectators, that I now may be
    In fair Bohemia; and remember well,
    I mentioned[5] a son o' the king's, which Florizel

---

[1] *leave the growth . . . wide gap*] leave unexamined the progress of time that fills up that wide gap (of sixteen years).

[2] *in one self-born hour*] in one hour my own creation.

[3] *Now seems to it*] Now seems stale in comparison with the "glistering of this present."

[4] *imagine me*] "Me" is here the ethical dative, as in such phrases as "bethink me."

[5] *I mentioned*] Thus the Folios. Mention has been made of Polixenes's young prince by both Polixenes and Leontes, and to these remarks Time here seems to refer, vaguely assuming responsibility for their utterance.

I now name to you; and with speed so pace[6]
To speak of Perdita, now grown in grace
Equal with wondering:[7] what of her ensues
I list not prophesy; but let Time's news
Be known when 't is brought forth. A shepherd's daughter,
And what to her adheres, which follows after,
Is the argument of Time. Of this allow,
If ever you have spent time worse ere now;
If never, yet that Time himself doth say
He wishes earnestly you never may.   [*Exit.*

SCENE II. *Bohemia—The Palace of Polixenes*

Enter POLIXENES *and* CAMILLO

POL.   I pray thee, good Camillo, be no more importunate: 't is a sickness denying thee any thing; a death to grant this.

CAM.   It is fifteen[1] years since I saw my country: though I have for the most part been aired[2] abroad, I desire to lay my bones there. Besides, the penitent king, my master, hath sent for me; to whose feeling sorrows I might be some allay, or I o'erween to think so, which is another spur to my departure.

POL.   As thou lovest me, Camillo, wipe not out the rest of thy services by leaving me now: the need I have of thee, thine own goodness hath made; better not to have had thee than thus to want thee: thou, having made me businesses, which none without thee can sufficiently manage, must either stay to execute them thyself, or take away with thee the very services thou hast done; which if I have not enough considered, as too much I cannot, to be more thankful to thee shall be my study; and my profit therein, the heaping friendships.[3] Of that fatal country, Sicilia, prithee speak no more; whose very naming punishes me with the remembrance of that penitent, as thou callest him, and reconciled king, my brother; whose loss of his most precious queen and children are even now to be afresh lamented. Say to me, when sawest thou the Prince Florizel, my son? Kings are no less unhappy, their issue not

---

[6]*with speed so pace*] with equal haste go forward.
[7]*Equal with wondering*] To an extent that justifies no less wonder or admiration.

---

[1]*fifteen*] Thus the Folios. But *sixteen* years is thrice stated elsewhere to be the length of time that elapses between the first and second parts of the play.
[2]*have . . . been aired*] have breathed air, lived.
[3]*friendships*] friendly services.

being gracious,[4] than they are in losing them when they have approved their virtues.

CAM.   Sir, it is three days since I saw the prince. What his happier affairs may be, are to me unknown: but I have missingly[5] noted, he is of late much retired from court and is less frequent to his princely exercises than formerly he hath appeared.

POL.   I have considered so much, Camillo, and with some care; so far, that I have eyes under my service which look upon his removedness;[6] from whom I have this intelligence, that he is seldom from the house of a most homely shepherd; a man, they say that from very nothing, and beyond the imagination of his neighbours, is grown into an unspeakable estate.

CAM.   I have heard, sir, of such a man, who hath a daughter of most rare note: the report of her is extended more than can be thought to begin from such a cottage.

POL.   That 's likewise part of my intelligence; but, I fear, the angle[7] that plucks our son thither. Thou shalt accompany us to the place; where we will, not appearing what we are, have some question with the shepherd; from whose simplicity I think it not uneasy to get the cause of my son's resort thither. Prithee, be my present partner in this business, and lay aside the thoughts of Sicilia.

CAM.   I willingly obey your command.

POL.   My best Camillo! We must disguise ourselves.   [*Exeunt.*

SCENE III. *A Road Near the Shepherd's Cottage*

Enter AUTOLYCUS, *singing*

> When daffodils begin to peer,
>   With heigh! the doxy[1] over the dale,
> Why, then comes in the sweet o' the year;[2]
>   For the red blood reigns in the winter's pale.[3]

---

[4]*gracious*] in a state of grace, well conducted.
[5]*missingly*] missing him, feeling his absence.
[6]*eyes . . . removedness*] spies who watch him in his withdrawal from court.
[7]*but, I fear, the angle*] but I fear she is the hook and line, or the attraction. "Angle" here means "fishing-rod."

---

[1]*doxy*] beggar's mistress.
[2]*sweet o' the year*] Beaumont and Fletcher, in *A Wife for a Month*, II, i, applies the phrase to the month of April.
[3]*red blood . . . pale*] the red blood of spring conquers the province of snow-coloured winter; "pale" is used in the double sense of "paleness," and of "settlement" or "province."

The white sheet bleaching on the hedge,
  With heigh! the sweet birds, O, how they sing!
Doth set my pugging[4] tooth on edge;
  For a quart of ale is a dish for a king

The lark, that tirra-lyra chants,
  With heigh! with heigh! the thrush and the jay,
Are summer songs for me and my aunts,[5]
  While we lie tumbling in the hay.

I have served Prince Florizel and in my time wore three-pile;[6] but now I am out of service:

But shall I go mourn for that, my dear?
  The pale moon shines by night:
And when I wander here and there,
  I then do most go right.

If tinkers may have leave to live,
  And bear the sow-skin budget,[7]
Then my account I well may give,
  And in the stocks avouch it.

My traffic is sheets; when the kite builds, look to lesser linen.[8] My father named me Autolycus; who being, as I am, littered under Mercury, was likewise a snapper-up of unconsidered trifles. With die and drab I purchased this caparison,[9] and my revenue is the silly cheat. Gallows and knock[10] are too powerful on the highway: beating and hanging are terrors to me: for the life to come, I sleep out the thought[11] of it. A prize! a prize!

Enter Clown

---

[4]*pugging*] thievish. Cf. "puggard," a cant term for a thief.

[5]*aunts*] a slang word of the same significance as "doxy" (see footnote 1).

[6]*three-pile*] the most costly kind of velvet, worn only by persons of consequence.

[7]*sow-skin budget*] pouch or wallet of pigskin.

[8]*My traffic . . . linen*] Autolycus's business is the theft of sheets, of larger linen. The kite, when building its nest, takes smaller pieces of linen, which only then need special guarding. According to Ovid, *Metamorphoses*, XI, 313–315, a work which Shakespeare knew well, Autolycus was a son of Mercury, "furtum ingeniosus ad omne . . . patriæ non degener artis." In Golding's translation it is said that he "proved a wily pie And such fellow as in theft and filching had no pew."

[9]*With die and drab . . . caparison*] By means of gaming and going with loose women I acquired these rags.

[10]*knock*] a reference to the blows to which the highwayman is liable from those whom he assaults.

[11]*I sleep out the thought*] I drown in sleep the thought.

CLO.   Let me see: every 'leven wether tods;[12] every tod yields pound
and odd shilling; fifteen hundred shorn, what comes the wool to?

AUT. [*Aside*]   If the springe[13] hold, the cock 's mine.

CLO.   I cannot do 't without counters. Let me see; what am I to buy
for our sheep-shearing feast? Three pound of sugar; five pound of
currants; rice—what will this sister of mine do with rice? But my
father hath made her mistress of the feast, and she lays it on. She
hath made me four and twenty nosegays for the shearers, three-
man songmen[14] all, and very good ones; but they are most of them
means[15] and bases; but one puritan amongst them, and he sings
psalms to hornpipes.[16] I must have saffron to colour the warden
pies;[17] mace; dates, none, that 's out of my note;[18] nutmegs, seven;
a race[19] or two of ginger, but that I may beg; four pound of prunes,
and as many of raisins o' the sun.[20]

AUT.   O that ever I was born!   [*Grovelling on the ground.*

CLO.   I' the name of me—

AUT.   O, help me, help me! pluck but off these rags; and then,
death, death!

CLO.   Alack, poor soul! thou hast need of more rags to lay on thee,
rather than have these off.

AUT.   O sir, the loathsomeness of them offends me more than the
stripes I have received, which are mighty ones and millions.

CLO.   Alas, poor man! a million of beating may come to a great
matter.

AUT.   I am robbed, sir, and beaten; my money and apparel ta'en from
me, and these detestable things put upon me.

CLO.   What, by a horseman, or a footman?

AUT.   A footman, sweet sir, a footman.

CLO.   Indeed, he should be a footman by the garments he has left
with thee: if this be a horseman's coat, it hath seen very hot service. Lend me thy hand, I 'll help thee: come, lend me thy hand.

                                                    [*Helping him up.*

[12]*every 'leven wether tods*] every eleven sheep will produce a tod or twenty-eight pounds
of wool.

[13]*springe*] trap, snare.

[14]*three-man songmen*] singers of catches. A "three-man song" was a catch in three parts.

[15]*means*] the parts between the tenor and the treble. There is a pun here, implying that
the songmen are "mean" fellows of no account.

[16]*to hornpipes*] to the lively tunes commonly played on hornpipes.

[17]*warden pies*] pies of warden, or baking, pears.

[18]*out of my note*] It is questionable whether the clown would be reading from a written
list. It probably means here that the item "dates" is not in the directions, which he is
repeating from memory.

[19]*race*] root. Cf. old French *raïs*, Spanish *raiz*, and Latin *radix*.

[20]*raisins o' the sun*] the ordinary raisin which is dried in the sun.

Aut.   O, good sir, tenderly, O!

Clo.   Alas, poor soul!

Aut.   O, good sir, softly, good sir! I fear, sir, my shoulder-blade is out.

Clo.   How now! canst stand?

Aut.   Softly, dear sir [*picks his pocket*]; good sir, softly. You ha' done me a charitable office.

Clo.   Dost lack any money? I have a little money for thee.

Aut.   No, good sweet sir; no, I beseech you, sir: I have a kinsman not past three quarters of a mile hence, unto whom I was going; I shall there have money, or any thing I want: offer me no money, I pray you; that kills my heart.

Clo.   What manner of fellow was he that robbed you?

Aut.   A fellow, sir, that I have known to go about with troll-my-dames:[21] I knew him once a servant of the prince: I cannot tell, good sir, for which of his virtues it was, but he was certainly whipped out of the court.

Clo.   His vices, you would say; there 's no virtue whipped out of the court: they cherish it to make it stay there; and yet it will no more but abide.[22]

Aut.   Vices I would say, sir. I know this man well: he hath been since an ape-bearer;[23] then a process-server, a bailiff; then he compassed a motion of the Prodigal Son,[24] and married a tinker's wife within a mile where my land and living lies; and, having flown over many knavish professions, he settled only in rogue: some call him Autolycus.

Clo.   Out upon him! prig,[25] for my life, prig: he haunts wakes, fairs and bear-baitings.

Aut.   Very true, sir; he, sir, he; that 's the rogue that put me into this apparel.

Clo.   Not a more cowardly rogue in all Bohemia: if you had but looked big and spit at him, he 'ld have run.

Aut.   I must confess to you, sir, I am no fighter: I am false of heart that way; and that he knew, I warrant him.

Clo.   How do you now?

Aut.   Sweet sir, much better than I was; I can stand and walk: I will even take my leave of you, and pace softly towards my kinsman's.

---

[21]*troll-my-dames*] A French game resembling nine holes or bagatelle, which was called "trou-madame," would seem to have suggested this invented term for light women.

[22]*will no more but abide*] will barely stay.

[23]*ape-bearer*] travelling showman with a performing ape.

[24]*a motion of the Prodigal Son*] Puppet shows of this and other scriptural tales were popular exhibitions at the time.

[25]*prig*] slang word for a thief.

CLO.   Shall I bring thee on the way?
AUT.   No, good-faced sir; no, sweet sir.
CLO.   Then fare thee well: I must go buy spices for our sheep-
       shearing.
AUT.   Prosper you, sweet sir! [*Exit* Clown.] Your purse is not hot
       enough to purchase your spice. I 'll be with you at your sheep-
       shearing too: if I make not this cheat bring out another and the
       shearers prove sheep, let me be unrolled and my name put in the
       book of virtue![26]

SONG

Jog on, jog on, the foot-path way,
    And merrily hent[27] the stile-a:
A merry heart goes all the day,
    Your sad tires in a mile-a.[28]

SCENE IV. *The Shepherd's Cottage*

Enter FLORIZEL *and* PERDITA

FLO.   These your unusual weeds to each part of you
       Do give a life: no shepherdess, but Flora
       Peering in April's front.[1] This your sheep-shearing
       Is as a meeting of the petty gods,
       And you the queen on 't.
PER.   Sir, my gracious lord,
       To chide at your extremes[2] it not becomes me:
       O, pardon, that I name them! Your high self,
       The gracious mark o' the land, you have obscured
       With a swain's wearing, and me, poor lowly maid,
       Most goddess-like prank'd up: but that our feasts
       In every mess have folly and the feeders

---

[26]*unrolled and my name put in the book of virtue*] struck off the roll of thieves, struck
  out of the book of vice.
[27]*hent*] grip, take hold of (in order to vault over).
[28]*Jog on . . . a mile-a*] This was clearly a popular song of the day. The contemporary tune
  is found in Queen Elizabeth's *Virginal Book*, a manuscript in the Fitzwilliam
  Museum at Cambridge. In the miscellany called *An Antidote against Melancholy*,
  1661, Autolycus's lines are repeated without any author's name, together with a
  second stanza.

---

[1]*Peering in April's front*] Appearing at the beginning of April.
[2]*your extremes*] the extravagance of your conduct in disguising yourself.

Digest it with a custom,[3] I should blush
To see you so attired, sworn, I think,
To show myself a glass.[4]

FLO.   I bless the time
When my good falcon made her flight across
Thy father's ground.

PER.   Now Jove afford you cause!
To me the difference[5] forges dread; your greatness
Hath not been used to fear. Even now I tremble
To think your father, by some accident,
Should pass this way as you did: O, the Fates!
How would he look, to see his work, so noble,
Vilely bound up?[6] What would he say? Or how
Should I, in these my borrow'd flaunts, behold
The sternness of his presence?

FLO.   Apprehend
Nothing but jollity. The gods themselves,
Humbling their deities of love, have taken
The shapes of beasts upon them: Jupiter
Became a bull, and bellow'd; the green Neptune
A ram, and bleated; and the fire-robed god,
Golden Apollo, a poor humble swain,
As I seem now. Their transformations
Were never for a piece of beauty rarer,
Nor in a way[7] so chaste, since my desires
Run not before mine honour, nor my lusts
Burn hotter than my faith.

PER.   O, but, sir,
Your resolution cannot hold, when 't is
Opposed, as it must be, by the power of the king:
One of these two must be necessities,
Which then will speak, that you must change this purpose,
Or I my life.[8]

FLO.   Thou dearest Perdita,

---

[3]*our feasts . . . with a custom*] At every table or in every group, our feasts through every rank admit strange frolics, and the guests accept it all as customary. The necessary *it* following *digest* was first supplied in the Second Folio.

[4]*sworn . . . glass*] The prince seems, by his rustic disguise, to be fulfilling an oath to show her, as in a glass, her own dress.

[5]*the difference*] the difference of rank between us.

[6]*his work . . . bound up*] Florizel is compared with a fine piece of literature badly bound, clothed in an inferior binding.

[7]*Nor in a way*] The suggested emendation *Nor any way* is worth considering.

[8]*Or I my life*] Or I must convert my life or rank of rusticity into one of gentility.

With these forced thoughts, I prithee, darken not
The mirth o' the feast. Or I 'll be thine, my fair,
Or not my father's. For I cannot be
Mine own, nor any thing to any, if
I be not thine. To this I am most constant,
Though destiny say no. Be merry, gentle;
Strangle such thoughts as these with any thing
That you behold the while. Your guests are coming:
Lift up your countenance, as it were the day
Of celebration of that nuptial which
We two have sworn shall come.

PER.   O lady Fortune,
Stand you auspicious!

FLO.   See, your guests approach:
Address yourself to entertain them sprightly,
And let 's be red with mirth.

Enter Shepherd, Clown, MOPSA, DORCAS, *and others, with* POLIXENES
and CAMILLO *disguised*

SHEP.   Fie, daughter! when my old wife lived, upon
This day she was both pantler,[9] butler, cook,
Both dame and servant; welcomed all, served all;
Would sing her song and dance her turn; now here,
At upper end o' the table, now i' the middle;
On his shoulder, and his; her face o' fire
With labour and the thing she took to quench it,
She would to each one sip. You are retired,
As if you were a feasted one and not
The hostess of the meeting: pray you, bid
These unknown friends to 's welcome; for it is
A way to make us better friends, more known.
Come, quench your blushes and present yourself
That which you are, mistress o' the feast: come on,
And bid us welcome to your sheep-shearing,
As your good flock shall prosper.

PER. [*To* POL.]   Sir, welcome:
It is my father's will I should take on me
The hostess-ship o' the day. [*To* CAM.] You 're welcome, sir.
Give me those flowers there, Dorcas. Reverend sirs,
For you there 's rosemary and rue; these keep
Seeming and savour all the winter long:
Grace and remembrance be to you both,

---

[9]*pantler*] pantry-man.

And welcome to our shearing!

POL.   Shepherdess,
A fair one are you, well you fit our ages
With flowers of winter.

PER.   Sir, the year growing ancient,
Not yet on summer's death, nor on the birth
Of trembling winter, the fairest flowers o' the season
Are our carnations and streak'd gillyvors,[10]
Which some call nature's bastards: of that kind
Our rustic garden 's barren; and I care not
To get slips of them.

POL.   Wherefore, gentle maiden,
Do you neglect them?

PER.   For I have heard it said
There is an art which in their piedness shares
With great creating nature.[11]

POL.   Say there be;
Yet nature is made better by no mean,
But nature makes that mean: so, over that art
Which you say adds to nature, is an art
That nature makes. You see, sweet maid, we marry
A gentler scion to the wildest stock,
And make conceive a bark of baser kind
By bud of nobler race: this is an art
Which does mend nature, change it rather, but
The art itself is nature.

PER.   So it is.

POL.   Then make your garden rich in gillyvors,
And do not call them bastards.

PER.   I 'll not put
The dibble[12] in earth to set one slip of them;
No more than were I painted I would wish
This youth should say 't were well, and only therefore
Desire to breed by me. Here 's flowers for you;
Hot lavender, mints,[13] savory, marjoram;

---

[10]*gillyvors*] a corruption of the French "girofle." The name is commonly bestowed on various kinds of pinks or carnations. Possibly Perdita credits the "streak'd" flower with a bad character because its colouring suggests the painting in which immodest women indulged.

[11]*For I . . . nature*] Because Perdita has heard of an art which competes with nature in creating the gillyvors' variegation of colour.

[12]*dibble*] a small sharp hoe.

[13]*mints*] usually found in the plural in Elizabethan authors, owing to the various species of the herb in common use.

    The marigold,[14] that goes to bed wi' the sun
    And with him rises weeping: these are flowers
    Of middle summer, and I think they are given
    To men of middle age. You 're very welcome.
CAM.   I should leave grazing, were I of your flock,
    And only live by gazing.
PER.   Out, alas!
    You 'ld be so lean, that blasts of January
    Would blow you through and through. Now, my fair'st friend,
    I would I had some flowers o' the spring that might
    Become your time of day; and yours, and yours,
    That wear upon your virgin branches yet
    Your maidenheads growing: O Proserpina,
    For the flowers now, that frighted thou let'st fall
    From Dis's waggon![15] daffodils,
    That come before the swallow dares, and take[16]
    The winds of March with beauty; violets dim,
    But sweeter than the lids of Juno's eyes
    Or Cytherea's breath; pale primroses,
    That die unmarried, ere they can behold
    Bright Phœbus in his strength, a malady
    Most incident to maids; bold oxlips and
    The crown imperial;[17] lilies of all kinds,
    The flower-de-luce[18] being one! O, these I lack,
    To make you garlands of; and my sweet friend,
    To strew him o'er and o'er!
FLO.   What, like a corse?
PER.   No, like a bank for love to lie and play on;
    Not like a corse; or if, not to be buried,
    But quick and in mine arms. Come, take your flowers:
    Methinks I play as I have seen them do
    In Whitsun pastorals: sure this robe of mine
    Does change my disposition.
FLO.   What you do
    Still betters what is done. When you speak, sweet,

---

[14]*marigold*] probably the garden marigold, *calendula officinalis*.

[15]*O Proserpina . . . Dis's waggon*] A reminiscence of Ovid's story in *Metamorphoses*, V. 359 *seq.*, of the rape of Proserpina, who, affrighted by the approach of Pluto's chariot, lets fall from her lap the flowers she had gathered. Cf. Golding's translation, "By chance *she let her lap slip downe and out her flowers went*," etc.

[16]*take*] bewitch, captivate. The usage survives in the modern colloquial epithet "taking."

[17]*crown imperial*] the fritillary, called *fritillaria imperialis*.

[18]*flower-de-luce*] The fleur de lys is usually identified with an iris, not with a lily.

I 'ld have you do it ever: when you sing,
I 'ld have you buy and sell so, so give alms,
Pray so: and, for the ordering your affairs,
To sing them too: when you do dance, I wish you
A wave o' the sea, that you might ever do
Nothing but that; move still, still so,
And own no other function: each your doing,
So singular in each particular,
Crowns what you are doing in the present deeds,
That all your acts are queens.[19]

PER.   O Doricles,
Your praises are too large: but that your youth,
And the true blood which peeps[20] fairly through 't,
Do plainly give you out an unstain'd shepherd,
With wisdom[21] I might fear, my Doricles,
You woo'd me the false way.

FLO.   I think you have
As little skill[22] to fear as I have purpose
To put you to 't.[23] But come; our dance, I pray:
Your hand, my Perdita: so turtles pair,
That never mean to part.

PER.   I 'll swear for 'em.

POL.   This is the prettiest low-born lass that ever
Ran on the green-sward: nothing she does or seems
But smacks of something greater than herself,
Too noble for this place.

CAM.   He tells her something
That makes her blood look out:[24] good sooth, she is
The queen of curds and cream.

CLO.   Come on, strike up!

DOR.   Mopsa must be your mistress: marry, garlic,
To mend her kissing with!

MOP.   Now, in good time![25]

---

[19]*each your doing . . . queens*] your manner of doing each thing, so unique in excellence
in every detail, crowns all that you are engaged in doing at the moment; each one of
your acts is of royal quality, deserves a queen's crown.

[20]*peeps*] Thus the Folios. The metre requires that "peeps" should be read as a dissylla-
ble. Capell and other editors insert *so* before *fairly*, on the metrical ground.

[21]*With wisdom*] On consideration.

[22]*skill*] reason, the outcome of skill or knowledge.

[23]*To put you to 't*] To give you occasion for it.

[24]*look out*] Theobald's correction of the Folio reading *looke on 't*. "Makes her blood look
out" means "calls up the blood in her cheeks," "makes her blush."

[25]*Now, in good time*] An ejaculation of surprise implying rebuke.

CLO.   Not a word, a word; we stand upon our manners.
     Come, strike up!

[*Music. Here a dance of* Shepherds *and* Shepherdesses.]

POL.   Pray, good shepherd, what fair swain is this   .
     Which dances with your daughter?
SHEP.   They call him Doricles; and boasts himself
     To have a worthy feeding:[26] but I have it
     Upon his own report and I believe it;
     He looks like sooth. He says he loves my daughter:
     I think so too; for never gazed the moon
     Upon the water, as he 'll stand and read
     As 't were my daughter's eyes: and, to be plain,
     I think there is not half a kiss to choose
     Who loves another best.
POL.   She dances featly.
SHEP.   So she does any thing; though I report it,
     That should be silent: if young Doricles
     Do light upon her, she shall bring him that
     Which he not dreams of.

Enter Servant

SERV.   O master, if you did but hear the pedlar at the door, you would
     never dance again after a tabor and pipe; no, the bagpipe could
     not move you: he sings several tunes faster than you 'll tell money;
     he utters them as he had eaten ballads and all men's ears grew to
     his tunes.
CLO.   He could never come better; he shall come in. I love a ballad
     but even too well, if it be doleful matter merrily set down, or a very
     pleasant thing indeed and sung lamentably.
SERV.   He hath songs for man or woman, of all sizes; no milliner[27] can
     so fit his customers with gloves: he has the prettiest love-songs for
     maids; so without bawdry, which is strange; with such delicate
     burthens of dildos and fadings,[28] "jump her and thump her;" and
     where some stretch-mouthed[29] rascal would, as it were, mean mis-
     chief and break a foul gap[30] into the matter, he makes the maid to

[26]*worthy feeding*] pasturage of value.
[27]*milliner*] here used by Shakespeare for a man who sells fancy articles.
[28]*dildos and fadings*] "Dildo" is a word often found in the nonsense refrains of popular
   songs. It was also used at times in a coarse sense, which added indelicate point to a
   vulgar song's burden. "Fadings," which is likewise found in the refrains of popular
   songs, was properly the name of a popular Irish dance.
[29]*stretch-mouthed*] broad-mouthed, foul-mouthed.
[30]*break a foul gap*] insert a coarse digression or parenthesis.

answer "Whoop, do me no harm, good man;"[31] puts him off,
slights him, with "Whoop, do me no harm, good man."

POL.   This is a brave fellow.

CLO.   Believe me, thou talkest of an admirable conceited fellow. Has
he any unbraided wares?[32]

SERV.   He hath ribbons of all the colours i' the rainbow; points[33] more
than all the lawyers in Bohemia can learnedly handle, though
they come to him by the gross: inkles, caddisses,[34] cambrics,
lawns: why, he sings 'em over as they were gods or goddesses; you
would think a smock were a she-angel, he so chants to the sleeve-
hand[35] and the work about the square on 't.[36]

CLO.   Prithee bring him in; and let him approach singing.

PER.   Forewarn him that he use no scurrilous words in 's tunes.

[*Exit* Servant.

CLO.   You have of these pedlars, that have more in them than you 'ld
think, sister.

PER.   Ay, good brother, or go about to think.

Enter AUTOLYCUS, *singing*

> Lawn as white as driven snow;
> Cypress black[37] as e'er was crow;
> Gloves as sweet as damask roses;[38]
> Masks for faces and for noses;
> Bugle bracelet, necklace amber,
> Perfume for a lady's chamber;
> Golden quoifs and stomachers,
> For my lads to give their dears;

---

[31]"*Whoop, do me no harm, good man*"] The burden of a coarse song, of which mention
is made in *The Famous History of Friar Bacon*. The tune is given in Corkine's *Ayres*,
1610, No. 20.

[32]*unbraided wares*] undamaged goods. For "braided ware" [*i.e.*, "damaged goods,"] see
Marston's *Scourge of Villainie*, Satire V. The proposed substitution of *embroidered* for
unbraided is needless.

[33]*points*] laces with metal tags.

[34]*inkles, caddisses*] linen tape, worsted tape.

[35]*sleeve-hand*] cuff or wristband.

[36]*work about the square on 't*] embroidery about the square-cut bosom front of the
smock.

[37]*Cypress black*] Black crape. *Cyprus* was substituted for *cypress* by Rowe on the ground
that the fabric may have been manufactured from cloth or satin, which is often stated
to have been imported from Cyprus in Shakespeare's day. Less satisfactory is the sug-
gestion that the reference is to the cypress tree, from which it is only known that ropes
and matting were made.

[38]*Gloves as sweet . . . roses*] Perfumed gloves were in fashion.

    Pins and poking-sticks[39] of steel,
    What maids lack from head to heel:
    Come buy of me, come; come buy, come buy;
    Buy, lads, or else your lasses cry:
    Come buy.[40]

CLO. If I were not in love with Mopsa, thou shouldst take no money of me; but being enthralled as I am, it will also be the bondage of certain ribbons and gloves.

MOP. I was promised them against the feast; but they come not too late now.

DOR. He hath promised you more than that, or there be liars.

MOP. He hath paid you all he promised you: may be, he has paid you more, which will shame you to give him again.

CLO. Is there no manners left among maids? will they wear their plackets[41] where they should bear their faces? Is there not milking-time, when you are going to bed, or kiln-hole,[42] to whistle off these secrets, but you must be tittle-tattling before all our guests? 't is well they are whispering: clamour[43] your tongues, and not a word more.

MOP. I have done. Come, you promised me a tawdry-lace[44] and a pair of sweet gloves.

CLO. Have I not told thee how I was cozened by the way and lost all my money?

AUT. And indeed, sir, there are cozeners abroad; therefore it behoves men to be wary.

CLO. Fear not thou, man, thou shalt lose nothing here.

AUT. I hope so, sir; for I have about me many parcels of charge.

CLO. What hast here? ballads?

MOP. Pray now, buy some: I love a ballad in print o' life,[45] for then we are sure they are true.

---

[39]*poking-sticks*] steel rods to be heated in the fire wherewith to adjust and stiffen the plaits of ruffs.

[40]*Come buy of me, come, etc.*] The music, with words, of this song is found in John Wilson's *Cheerfull Ayres*, 1660.

[41]*plackets*] The word is used in many senses, some of which are indelicate. Here it means woman's undergarments. The clown asks in effect: "Will they wear their undergarments outside?" "Will they disclose everything?"

[42]*kiln-hole*] the fireplace for making malt, a favourite place for gossiping.

[43]*clamour*] apparently a rare intensitive derived from "clam" or "clem," which is found in contemporary authors in the sense of "stifle" or "stop." It seems desirable to adopt the proposed spelling *clammer*.

[44]*tawdry-lace*] a rustic necklace.

[45]*o' life*] The Folios read a *life*. But an imprecation is clearly intended, equivalent to "i' faith," "in truth;" "a' life" or "o' life" (*i.e.*, "upon my life") is often used thus in Elizabethan English.

AUT. Here 's one to a very doleful tune, how a usurer's wife was brought to bed of twenty money-bags at a burthen, and how she longed to eat adders' heads and toads carbonadoed.[46]

MOP. Is it true, think you?

AUT. Very true, and but a month old.

DOR. Bless me from marrying a usurer!

AUT. Here 's the midwife's name to 't, one Mistress Tale-porter, and five or six honest wives that were present. Why should I carry lies abroad?

MOP. Pray you now, buy it.

CLO. Come on, lay it by: and let 's first see more ballads; we 'll buy the other things anon.

AUT. Here 's another ballad of a fish, that appeared upon the coast, on Wednesday the fourscore of April, forty thousand fathom above water, and sung this ballad against the hard hearts of maids: it was thought she was a woman, and was turned into a cold fish for she would not exchange flesh with one that loved her: the ballad is very pitiful and as true.

DOR. Is it true too, think you?

AUT. Five justices' hands at it, and witnesses more than my pack will hold.

CLO. Lay it by too: another.

AUT. This is a merry ballad, but a very pretty one.

MOP. Let 's have some merry ones.

AUT. Why, this is a passing merry one and goes to the tune of "Two maids wooing a man:" there 's scarce a maid westward but she sings it; 't is in request, I can tell you.

MOP. We can both sing it: if thou 'lt bear a part, thou shalt hear; 't is in three parts.

DOR. We had the tune on 't a month ago.

AUT. I can bear my part; you must know 't is my occupation: have at it with you.

SONG

A. Get you hence, for I must go
Where it fits not you to know.
    D. Whither? M. O, whither? D. Whither?

M. It becomes thy oath full well,
Thou to me thy secrets tell:
    D. Me too, let me go thither.

---

[46]*carbonadoed*] often used of a piece of meat cut across or slashed for broiling.

>   M.   Or thou goest to the grange or mill:
>   D.   If to either, thou dost ill.
>   A.   Neither. D.   What, neither? A.   Neither.
>   D.   Thou hast sworn my love to be;
>   M.   Thou hast sworn it more to me:
>   Then whither goest? say, whither?

CLO.   We 'll have this song out anon by ourselves: my father and the
gentlemen are in sad talk,[47] and we 'll not trouble them. Come,
bring away thy pack after me. Wenches, I 'll buy for you both.
Pedlar, let 's have the first choice. Follow me, girls.

                                     [*Exit with* DORCAS *and* MOPSA.

AUT.   And you shall pay well for 'em.   [*Follows singing.*

>   Will you buy any tape,
>   Or lace for your cape,
>   My dainty duck, my dear-a?
>   Any silk, any thread,
>   Any toys for your head,
>   Of the new'st, and finest, finest wear-a?
>   Come to the pedlar;
>   Money 's a medler,
>   That doth utter[48] all men's ware-a.   [*Exit.*

Re-enter Servant

SERV.   Master, there is three carters, three shepherds, three neat-
herds, three swine-herds, that have made themselves all men of
hair, they call themselves Saltiers,[49] and they have a dance which
the wenches say is a gallimaufry[50] of gambols, because they are
not in 't; but they themselves are o' the mind, if it be not too rough
for some that know little but bowling,[51] it will please plentifully.

SHEP.   Away! we 'll none on 't: here has been too much homely fool-
ery already. I know, sir, we weary you.

POL.   You weary those that refresh us: pray, let 's see these four threes
of herdsmen.

SERV.   One three of them, by their own report, sir, hath danced before

---

[47]*sad talk*] serious, earnest talk.

[48]*a medler, That doth utter*] an agent that puts into circulation; "medler" is used in a
good sense here.

[49]*men of hair . . . Saltiers*] men dressed in hairy skins of goats or other animals. "Saltiers"
is a punning mispronunciation of "satyrs," in which characters the peasants perform
their dance. Literally, "saltiers" could only mean "saultiers," "vaulters," "somersault
throwers."

[50]*gallimaufry*] medley.

[51]*bowling*] the gentle game of bowls on a smooth green.

the king; and not the worst of the three but jumps twelve foot and
a half by the squier.[52]

SHEP. Leave your prating: since these good men are pleased, let them
come in; but quickly now.

SERV. Why, they stay at door, sir. [*Exit.*

[*Here a dance of twelve* Satyrs.]

POL. O, father, you 'll know more of that hereafter.
[*To* CAM.] Is it not too far gone? 'T is time to part them.
He 's simple and tells much. How now, fair shepherd!
Your heart is full of something that does take
Your mind from feasting. Sooth, when I was young
And handed[53] love as you do, I was wont
To load my she with knacks: I would have ransack'd
The pedlar's silken treasury and have pour'd it
To her acceptance; you have let him go
And nothing marted with him. If your lass
Interpretation should abuse[54] and call this
Your lack of love or bounty, you were straited
For a reply, at least if you make a care
Of happy holding her.

FLO.   Old sir, I know
She prizes not such trifles as these are:
The gifts she looks from me are pack'd and lock'd
Up in my heart; which I have given already,
But not deliver'd. O, hear me breathe my life
Before this ancient sir, who, it should seem,
Hath sometime loved! I take thy hand, this hand,
As soft as dove's down and as white as it,
Or Ethiopian's tooth, or the fann'd snow that 's bolted[55]
By the northern blasts twice o'er.

POL.   What follows this?
How prettily the young swain seems to wash
The hand was fair before! I have put you out:
But to your protestation; let me hear
What you profess.

FLO.   Do, and be witness to 't.

POL. And this my neighbour too?

---

[52]*squier*] from the French "esquierre," the mason's or carpenter's measuring rule or
    square.
[53]*handed*] touched or treated. The proposed substitution of *handled* is needless.
[54]*Interpretation should abuse*] Make a wrong interpretation of your conduct.
[55]*bolted*] sifted.

FLO.   And he, and more
          Than he, and men, the earth, the heavens, and all:
          That, were I crown'd the most imperial monarch,
          Thereof most worthy, were I the fairest youth
          That ever made eye swerve, had force and knowledge
          More than was ever man's, I would not prize them
          Without her love; for her employ them all;
          Commend[56] them and condemn them to her service
          Or to their own perdition.
POL.   Fairly offer'd.
CAM.   This shows a sound affection.
SHEP.   But, my daughter,
          Say you the like to him?
PER.   I cannot speak
          So well, nothing so well; no, nor mean better:
          By the pattern of mine own thoughts I cut out[57]
          The purity of his.
SHEP.   Take hands, a bargain!
          And, friends unknown, you shall bear witness to 't:
          I give my daughter to him, and will make
          Her portion equal his.
FLO.   O, that must be
          I' the virtue of your daughter: one being dead,
          I shall have more than you can dream of yet;
          Enough then for your wonder. But, come on.
          Contract us 'fore these witnesses.
SHEP.   Come, your hand;
          And, daughter, yours.
POL.   Soft, swain, awhile, beseech you;
          Have you a father?
FLO.   I have: but what of him?
POL.   Knows he of this?
FLO.   He neither does nor shall.
POL.   Methinks a father
          Is at the nuptial of his son a guest
          That best becomes the table. Pray you once more,
          Is not your father grown incapable
          Of reasonable affairs? is he not stupid
          With age and altering rheums?[58] can he speak? hear?

[56]*Commend*] Commit.
[57]*cut out*] a common term in dressmaking.
[58]*altering rheums*] rheumatic affections, which change a man's disposition or reduce his
    bodily power.

Know man from man? dispute his own estate?[59]
Lies he not bed-rid? and again does nothing
But what he did being childish?

FLO.   No, good sir;
He has his health and ampler strength indeed
Than most have of his age.

POL.   By my white beard,
You offer him, if this be so, a wrong
Something unfilial: reason my son[60]
Should choose himself a wife, but as good reason
The father, all whose joy is nothing else
But fair posterity, should hold some counsel
In such a business.

FLO.   I yield all this;
But for some other reasons, my grave sir,
Which 't is not fit you know, I not acquaint
My father of this business.

POL.   Let him know 't.

FLO.   He shall not.

POL.   Prithee, let him.

FLO.   No, he must not.

SHEP.   Let him, my son: he shall not need to grieve
At knowing of thy choice.

FLO.   Come, come, he must not.
Mark our contract.

POL.   Mark your divorce, young sir,
                                    [*Discovering himself.*

Whom son I dare not call; thou art too base
To be acknowledged: thou a sceptre's heir,
That thus affects a sheep-hook! Thou old traitor,
I am sorry that by hanging thee I can
But shorten thy life one week. And thou, fresh piece
Of excellent witchcraft, who of force must know
The royal fool thou copest with, —

SHEP.   O, my heart!

POL.   I 'll have thy beauty scratch'd with briers, and made
More homely than thy state. For thee, fond boy,
If I may ever know thou dost but sigh
That thou no more shalt see this knack,[61] as never
I mean thou shalt, we 'll bar thee from succession;

---

[59]*dispute his own estate*] discuss thy affairs.
[60]*reason my son*] there is reason that my son.
[61]*knack*] toy, or plaything.

Not hold thee of our blood, no, not our kin,
Far[62] than Deucalion[63] off: mark thou my words:
Follow us to the court. Thou churl, for this time,
Though full of our displeasure, yet we free thee
From the dead[64] blow of it. And you, enchantment,—
Worthy enough a herdsman; yea, him too,
That makes himself, but for our honour therein,
Unworthy thee,—if ever henceforth thou
These rural latches to his entrance open.
Or hoop[65] his body more with thy embraces,
I will devise a death as cruel for thee
As thou art tender to 't.   [*Exit.*

PER.   Even here undone!
I was not much afeard; for once or twice
I was about to speak and tell him plainly,
The selfsame sun that shines upon his court
Hides not his visage from our cottage, but
Looks on alike.[66] Will 't please you, sir, be gone?
I told you what would come of this: beseech you,
Of your own state take care: this dream of mine,—
Being now awake, I 'll queen it no inch farther,
But milk my ewes and weep.

CAM.   Why, how now, father!
Speak ere thou diest.

SHEP.   I cannot speak, nor think,
Nor dare to know that which I know. O sir!
You have undone a man of fourscore three,
That thought to fill his grave in quiet; yea,
To die upon the bed my father died,
To lie close by his honest bones: but now
Some hangman must put on my shroud and lay me
Where no priest shovels in dust.[67] O cursed wretch,
That knew'st this was the prince, and wouldst adventure
To mingle faith with him! Undone! undone!
If I might die within this hour, I have lived
To die when I desire.   [*Exit.*

---

[62]*Far*] Sometimes used as the comparative "farther," like "near" for "nearer."
[63]*Deucalion*] Deucalion, the Noah of classical mythology, is one of the heroes of Ovid's
    Metamorphoses, I, 313 *seq.*
[64]*dead*] deadly, fatal. The proposed change *dread*, though ingenious, is unnecessary.
[65]*hoop*] Pope's correction for the Folio misprint *hope.*
[66]*Looks on alike*] The phrase is still used as an intransitive verb (of an idle spectator).
[67]*Where no priest shovels in dust*] Without any burial service. In the old liturgies the
    priest is directed to fling earth into the grave.

FLO.   . Why look you so upon me?
    I am but sorry, not afeard; delay'd,
    But nothing alter'd: what I was, I am:
    More straining on for plucking back, not following
    My leash unwillingly.

CAM.   Gracious my lord,
    You know your father's[68] temper: at this time
    He will allow no speech, which I do guess
    You do not purpose to him; and as hardly
    Will he endure your sight as yet, I fear:
    Then, till the fury of his highness settle,
    Come not before him.

FLO.   I not purpose it.
    I think, Camillo?

CAM.   Even he, my lord.

PER.   How often have I told you 't would be thus!
    How often said, my dignity would last
    But till 't were known!

FLO.   It cannot fail but by
    The violation of my faith; and then
    Let nature crush the sides o' the earth together
    And mar the seeds within! Lift up thy looks:
    From my succession wipe me, father, I
    Am heir to my affection.

CAM.   Be advised.

FLO.   I am, and by my fancy:[69] if my reason
    Will thereto be obedient, I have reason;
    If not, my senses, better pleased with madness,
    Do bid it welcome.

CAM.   This is desperate, sir.

FLO.   So call it: but it does fulfil my vow;
    I needs must think it honesty. Camillo,
    Not for Bohemia, nor the pomp that may
    Be thereat glean'd; for all the sun sees, or
    The close earth wombs, or the profound seas hide
    In unknown fathoms, will I break my oath
    To this my fair beloved: therefore, I pray you,
    As you have ever been my father's honour'd friend,
    When he shall miss me,—as, in faith, I mean not
    To see him any more,—cast your good counsels

[68]*your father's*] The First Folio misprints *my father's*. The Second Folio made the
  correction.
[69]*fancy*] love.

Upon his passion: let myself and fortune
Tug for the time to come.[70] This you may know
And so deliver, I am put to sea
With her whom here I cannot hold on shore;
And most opportune to our need[71] I have
A vessel rides fast by, but not prepared
For this design. What course I mean to hold
Shall nothing benefit your knowledge, nor
Concern me the reporting.

CAM.   O my lord!
I would your spirit were easier for advice,
Or stronger for your need.

FLO.   Hark, Perdita.   [*Drawing her aside.*
I 'll hear you by and by.

CAM.   He 's irremoveable,
Resolved for flight. Now were I happy, if
His going I could frame to serve my turn,
Save him from danger, do him love and honour,
Purchase the sight again of dear Sicilia
And that unhappy king, my master, whom
I so much thirst to see.

FLO.   Now, good Camillo;
I am so fraught with curious[72] business that
I leave out ceremony.

CAM.   Sir, I think
You have heard of my poor services, i' the love
That I have borne your father?

FLO.   Very nobly
Have you deserved: it is my father's music
To speak your deeds, not little of his care
To have them recompensed as thought on.

CAM.   Well, my lord,
If you may please to think I love the king,
And through him what is nearest to him, which is
Your gracious self, embrace but my direction,
If your more ponderous and settled project
May suffer alteration, on mine honour
I 'll point you where you shall have such receiving
As shall become your highness; where you may
Enjoy your mistress, from the whom, I see,

---

[70]*Tug for the time to come*] Fight it out henceforth, make a fight of it for the future.
[71]*our need*] Theobald's correction of the Folio reading *her need*.
[72]*curious*] involving care or embarrassment.

There 's no disjunction to be made, but by
As heavens forefend! your ruin; marry her,
And, with my best endeavours in your absence,
Your discontenting father strive to qualify[73]
And bring him up to liking.

FLO.   How, Camillo,
May this, almost a miracle, be done?
That I may call thee something more than man
And after that trust to thee.

CAM.   Have you thought on
A place whereto you 'll go?

FLO.   Not any yet:
But as the unthought-on accident is guilty
To[74] what we wildly do, so we profess
Ourselves to be the slaves of chance, and flies
Of every wind that blows.

CAM.   Then list to me:
This follows, if you will not change your purpose
But undergo this flight, make for Sicilia,
And there present yourself and your fair princess,
For so I see she must be, 'fore Leontes:
She shall be habited as it becomes
The partner of your bed. Methinks I see
Leontes opening his free arms and weeping
His welcomes forth; asks thee the son forgiveness,
As 't were i' the father's person; kisses the hands
Of your fresh princess; o'er and o'er divides him
'Twixt his unkindness and his kindness;[75] the one
He chides to hell and bids the other grow
Faster than thought or time.

FLO.   Worthy Camillo,
What colour for my visitation shall I
Hold up before him?

CAM.   Sent by the king your father
To greet him and to give him comforts. Sir,
The manner of your bearing towards him, with
What you as from your father shall deliver,
Things known betwixt us three, I 'll write you down:
The which shall point you forth at every sitting

---

[73]*discontenting . . . qualify*] discontented . . . mollify.
[74]*is guilty To*] is responsible for.
[75]*o'er and o'er divides him . . . kindness*] constantly divides his talk between his past unkindness and his present kindness.

What you must say; that he shall not perceive
But that you have your father's bosom there
And speak his very heart.
FLO.   I am bound to you:
There is some sap in this.
CAM.   A course more promising
Than a wild dedication of yourselves
To unpath'd waters, undream'd shores, most certain
To miseries enough: no hope to help you,
But as you shake off one[76] to take another:
Nothing so certain as your anchors, who
Do their best office, if they can but stay you
Where you 'll be loath to be: besides you know
Prosperity 's the very bond of love,
Whose fresh complexion and whose heart together
Affliction alters.
PER.   One of these is true:
I think affliction may subdue the cheek,
But not take in[77] the mind.
CAM.   Yea, say you so?
There shall not at your father's house these seven years
Be born another such.
FLO.   My good Camillo,
She is as forward of her breeding as
She is i' the rear o' her birth.
CAM.   I cannot say 't is pity
She lacks instructions, for she seems a mistress
To most that teach.
PER.   Your pardon, sir; for this
I 'll blush you thanks.
FLO.   My prettiest Perdita!
But O, the thorns we stand upon! Camillo,
Preserver of my father, now of me,
The medicine of our house, how shall we do?
We are not furnish'd like Bohemia's son,
Nor shall appear in Sicilia.
CAM.   My lord,
Fear none of this: I think you know my fortunes
Do all lie there: it shall be so my care
To have you royally appointed as if
The scene you play were mine. For instance, sir,

[76]*one*] one misery.
[77]*take in*] conquer, subdue.

That you may know you shall not want, one word.

> [*They talk aside.*

Re-enter AUTOLYCUS

AUT. Ha, ha! what a fool Honesty is! and Trust, his sworn brother,
a very simple gentleman! I have sold all my trumpery; not a
counterfeit stone, not a ribbon, glass, pomander,[78] brooch, table-
book,[79] ballad, knife, tape, glove, shoe-tie, bracelet, horn-ring, to
keep my pack from fasting: they throng who should buy first, as if
my trinkets had been hallowed and brought a benediction to the
buyer: by which means I saw whose purse was best in picture;[80]
and what I saw, to my good use I remembered. My clown, who
wants but something to be a reasonable man, grew so in love with
the wenches' song, that he would not stir his pettitoes[81] till he had
both tune and words; which so drew the rest of the herd to me,
that all their other senses stuck in ears: you might have pinched a
placket, it was senseless; 't was nothing to geld a codpiece of a
purse; I would have filed keys off that hung in chains: no hearing,
no feeling, but my sir's song, and admiring the nothing of it. So
that in this time of lethargy I picked and cut most of their festival
purses; and had not the old man come in with a whoo-bub[82]
against his daughter and the king's son and scared my choughs
from the chaff, I had not left a purse alive in the whole army.

[CAMILLO, FLORIZEL, *and* PERDITA *come forward.*]

CAM. Nay, but my letters, by this means being there
So soon as you arrive, shall clear that doubt.

FLO. And those that you 'll procure from King Leontes—

CAM. Shall satisfy your father.

PER.   Happy be you!
All that you speak shows fair.

CAM.   Who have we here?

> [*Seeing* AUTOLYCUS.

We 'll make an instrument of this; omit
Nothing may give us aid.

AUT. If they have overheard me now, why, hanging.

CAM. How now, good fellow! why shakest thou so?
Fear not, man; here 's no harm intended to thee.

---

[78]*pomander*] a ball of perfumes, or smelling-salts.
[79]*table-book*] tablets, memorandum book.
[80]*best in picture*] best in appearance, and therefore best for *picking*. A feeble pun.
[81]*pettitoes*] feet; probably "pig's trotters."
[82]*whoo-bub*] the old spelling of "hubbub."

AUT.   I am a poor fellow, sir.

CAM.   Why, be so still; here 's nobody will steal that from thee: yet for the outside of thy poverty we must make an exchange; therefore discase[83] thee instantly,—thou must think there 's a necessity in 't,—and change garments with this gentleman: though the pennyworth on his side be the worst, yet hold thee, there 's some boot.[84]

AUT.   I am a poor fellow, sir. [*Aside*] I know ye well enough.

CAM.   Nay, prithee, dispatch: the gentleman is half flayed[85] already.

AUT.   Are you in earnest, sir? [*Aside*] I smell the trick on 't.

FLO.   Dispatch, I prithee.

AUT.   Indeed, I have had earnest;[86] but I cannot with conscience take it.

CAM.   Unbuckle, unbuckle.

[FLORIZEL *and* AUTOLYCUS *exchange garments.*]

    Fortunate mistress,—let my prophecy[87]
    Come home to ye!—you must retire yourself
    Into some covert: take your sweetheart's hat
    And pluck it o'er your brows, muffle your face,
    Dismantle you, and, as you can, disliken
    The truth of your own seeming; that you may—
    For I do fear eyes over[88]—to shipboard
    Get undescried.

PER.   I see the play so lies
    That I must bear a part.

CAM.   No remedy.
    Have you done there?

FLO.   Should I now meet my father,
    He would not call me son.

CAM.   Nay, you shall have no hat.
                    [*Giving it to* PERDITA.
    Come, lady, come. Farewell, my friend.

AUT.   Adieu, sir.

FLO.   O Perdita, what have we twain forgot!
    Pray you, a word.

CAM. [*Aside*]   What I do next, shall be to tell the king
    Of this escape and whither they are bound;

---

[83]*discase*] undress.
[84]*boot*] advantage, recompense.
[85]*flayed*] stripped.
[86]*earnest*] earnest money.
[87]*my prophecy*] my prophetic use of the epithet "fortunate."
[88]*eyes over*] overlooking, spying eyes.

Wherein my hope is I shall so prevail
To force him after: in whose company
I shall review[89] Sicilia, for whose sight
I have a woman's longing.

FLO.   Fortune speed us!
Thus we set on, Camillo, to the sea-side.

CAM.   The swifter speed the better.

[*Exeunt* FLORIZEL, PERDITA, *and* CAMILLO.

AUT.   I understand the business, I hear it: to have an open ear, a quick
eye, and a nimble hand, is necessary for a cut-purse; a good nose
is requisite also, to smell out work for the other senses. I see this is
the time that the unjust man doth thrive. What an exchange had
this been without boot![90] What a boot is here with this exchange!
Sure the gods do this year connive at us, and we may do any thing
extempore. The prince himself is about a piece of iniquity, stealing away from his father with his clog at his heels: if I thought it
were a piece of honesty to acquaint the king withal, I would not
do 't: I hold it the more knavery to conceal it; and therein am I
constant to my profession.

Re-enter Clown *and* Shepherd

Aside, aside; here is more matter for a hot brain: every lane's end,
every shop, church, session, hanging, yields a careful man work.

CLO.   See, see; what a man you are now! There is no other way but to
tell the king she 's a changeling and none of your flesh and blood.

SHEP.   Nay, but hear me.

CLO.   Nay, but hear me.

SHEP.   Go to, then.

CLO.   She being none of your flesh and blood, your flesh and blood
has not offended the king; and so your flesh and blood is not to be
punished by him. Show those things you found about her, those
secret things, all but what she has with her: this being done, let the
law go whistle: I warrant you.

SHEP.   I will tell the king all, every word, yea, and his son's pranks too;
who, I may say, is no honest man, neither to his father nor to me,
to go about to make me the king's brother-in-law.

CLO.   Indeed, brother-in-law was the farthest off you could have been
to him and then your blood had been the dearer by I know how[91]
much an ounce.

---

[89]*review*] see again.
[90]*without boot*] without profit, recompense.
[91]*I know how*] Thus the Folios. Hanmer substituted *I know not how*, probably rightly.

AUT. [*Aside*]   Very wisely, puppies!

SHEP.   Well, let us to the king: there is that in this fardel will make him scratch his beard.

AUT. [*Aside*]   I know not what impediment this complaint may be to the flight of my master.

CLO.   Pray heartily he be at palace.

AUT. [*Aside*]   Though I am not naturally honest, I am so sometimes by chance: let me pocket up my pedlar's excrement. [*Takes off his false beard.*] How now, rustics! whither are you bound?

SHEP.   To the palace, an it like your worship.

AUT.   Your affairs there, what, with whom, the condition of that fardel, the place of your dwelling, your names, your ages, of what having, breeding, and any thing that is fitting to be known, discover.

CLO.   We are but plain fellows, sir.

AUT.   A lie; you are rough and hairy. Let me have no lying: it becomes none but tradesmen, and they often give us soldiers the lie:[92] but we pay them for it with stamped coin, not stabbing steel; therefore they do not give us the lie.

CLO.   Your worship had like to have given us one, if you had not taken yourself with the manner.[93]

SHEP.   Are you a courtier, an 't like you, sir?

AUT.   Whether it like me or no, I am a courtier. Seest thou not the air of the court in these enfoldings? hath not my gait in it the measure[94] of the court? receives not thy nose court-odour from me? reflect I not on thy baseness court-contempt? Thinkest thou, for that I insinuate, or toaze[95] from thee thy business, I am therefore no courtier? I am courtier cap-a-pe; and one that will either push on or pluck back thy business there: whereupon I command thee to open thy affair.

SHEP.   My business, sir, is to the king.

AUT.   What advocate hast thou to him?

SHEP.   I know not, an 't like you.

CLO.   Advocate 's the court-word for a pheasant:[96] say you have none.

SHEP.   None, sir; I have no pheasant, cock nor hen.

---

[92]*give us . . . the lie*] lie about their wares when selling them to us soldiers. "Give us the lie" is repeated at the end of the line in the ordinary sense of "flatly contradict us" (in the manner which provokes a challenge).

[93]*taken . . . with the manner*] caught in the act; a legal phrase.

[94]*the measure*] the stately pace.

[95]*insinuate, or toaze*] slily ingratiate oneself or drag (or rend). The form "toaze" is not met with elsewhere. It is apparently a variant of "touse" (*i.e.*, pull).

[96]*Advocate's . . . pheasant*] The clown imagines that "advocate" is the word used at court for the gift of game or pheasants, which suitors were in the habit of offering patrons or judges.

AUT. How blessed are we that are not simple men!
    Yet nature might have made me as these are,
    Therefore I will not disdain.

CLO. This cannot be but a great courtier.

SHEP. His garments are rich, but he wears them not handsomely.

CLO. He seems to be the more noble in being fantastical: a great man, I 'll warrant; I know by the picking on 's teeth.[97]

AUT. The fardel there? what 's i' the fardel? Wherefore that box?

SHEP. Sir, there lies such secrets in this fardel and box, which none must know but the king; and which he shall know within this hour, if I may come to the speech of him.

AUT. Age, thou hast lost thy labour.

SHEP. Why, sir?

AUT. The king is not at the palace; he is gone aboard a new ship to purge melancholy and air himself: for, if thou beest capable of things serious, thou must know the king is full of grief.

SHEP. So 't is said, sir; about his son, that should have married a shepherd's daughter.

AUT. If that shepherd be not in hand-fast,[98] let him fly: the curses he shall have, the tortures he shall feel, will break the back of man, the heart of monster.

CLO. Think you so, sir?

AUT. Not he alone shall suffer what wit can make heavy and vengeance bitter; but those that are germane[99] to him, though removed fifty times, shall all come under the hangman: which though it be great pity, yet it is necessary. An old sheep-whistling rogue, a ram-tender, to offer to have his daughter come into grace![100] Some say he shall be stoned; but that death is too soft for him, say I: draw our throne into a sheep-cote! all deaths are too few, the sharpest too easy.

CLO. Has the old man e'er a son, sir, do you hear, an 't like you, sir?

AUT. He has a son, who shall be flayed alive; then, 'nointed over with honey, set on the head of a wasp's nest; then stand till he be three quarters and a dram dead; then recovered again with aqua-vitæ or some other hot infusion; then, raw as he is, and in the hottest day prognostication proclaims,[101] shall he be set against a brick-wall,

[97]*I know . . . teeth*] An Elizabethan man of fashion made conspicuous play with his toothpick.

[98]*hand-fast*] custody. Properly "handfast" means "the custody of a friend who gives security for one's appearance;" this form of detention is technically known in law as "mainprise."

[99]*germane*] akin.

[100]*come into grace*] get into good society.

[101]*hottest day prognostication proclaims*] hottest day which is foretold in the almanac.

the sun looking with a southward eye upon him, where he is to behold him with flies blown to death.[102] But what talk we of these
traitorly rascals, whose miseries are to be smiled at, their offences
being so capital? Tell me, for you seem to be honest plain men,
what you have to the king: being something gently considered,[103]
I 'll bring you where he is aboard, tender your persons to his presence, whisper him in your behalfs; and if it be in man besides the
king to effect your suits, here is man shall do it.

CLO.   He seems to be of great authority: close with him, give him
gold; and though authority be a stubborn bear, yet he is oft led
by the nose with gold: show the inside of your purse to the outside of his hand, and no more ado. Remember "stoned," and
"flayed alive."

SHEP.   An 't please you, sir, to undertake the business for us, here is
that gold I have: I 'll make it as much more and leave this young
man in pawn till I bring it you.

AUT.   After I have done what I promised?

SHEP.   Ay, sir.

AUT.   Well, give me the moiety. Are you a party in this business?

CLO.   In some sort, sir: but though my case[104] be a pitiful one, I hope
I shall not be flayed out of it.

AUT.   O, that 's the case of the shepherd's son: hang him, he 'll be
made an example.

CLO.   Comfort, good comfort! We must to the king and show our
strange sights: he must know 't is none of your daughter nor my sister; we are gone else. Sir, I will give you as much as this old man
does when the business is performed, and remain, as he says, your
pawn till it be brought you.

AUT.   I will trust you. Walk before toward the seaside; go on the right
hand: I will but look upon the hedge and follow you.

CLO.   We are blest in this man, as I may say, even blest.

SHEP.   Let 's before as he bids us: he was provided to do us good.

                              [*Exeunt* Shepherd *and* Clown.

AUT.   If I had a mind to be honest, I see Fortune would not suffer me:
she drops booties in my mouth. I am courted now with a double
occasion, gold and a means to do the prince my master good;

---

[102]*He has a son . . . to death*] Boccaccio in the story (Day II, story 9), whence Shakespeare drew the main plot of *Cymbeline,* condemns the character, whom
Shakespeare calls Iachimo, to an almost identical series of torments.

[103]*being . . . considered*] bearing a good, gentlemanlike reputation.

[104]*case*] a pun on "case" in the double sense of "skin" and "dilemma."

which who knows how that may turn back[105] to my advancement? I will bring these two moles, these blind ones, aboard him: if he think it fit to shore them again and that the complaint they have to the king concerns him nothing, let him call me rogue for being so far officious; for I am proof against that title and what shame else belongs to 't. To him will I present them: there may be matter in it.   [*Exit.*

[105]*turn back*] recoil.

ACT V

Scene I. *A Room in Leontes' Palace*

Enter Leontes, Cleomenes, Dion, Paulina, *and* Servants

Cleomenes.   Sir, you have done enough, and have perform'd
    A saint-like sorrow: no fault could you make,
    Which you have not redeem'd; indeed, paid down
    More penitence than done trespass: at the last,
    Do as the heavens have done, forget your evil;
    With them forgive yourself.
Leon.   Whilst I remember
    Her and her virtues, I cannot forget
    My blemishes in them,[1] and so still think of
    The wrong I did myself: which was so much,
    That heirless it hath made my kingdom; and
    Destroy'd the sweet'st companion that e'er man
    Bred his hopes out of.
Paul.   True, too true,[2] my lord:
    If, one by one, you wedded all the world,
    Or from the all that are took something good,
    To make a perfect woman, she you kill'd
    Would be unparallel'd.
Leon.   I think so. Kill'd!
    She I kill'd! I did so: but thou strikest me
    Sorely, to say I did; it is as bitter
    Upon thy tongue as in my thought: now, good now,[3]
    Say so but seldom.
Cleo.   Not at all, good lady:

---

[1] *in them*] in regard to them.
[2] *True, too true*] The Folios make Leontes's speech end with *of, true,* and Paulina's begin with *Too true.* Theobald rearranged the words, with manifest advantage to sense and metre.
[3] *now, good now*] a plaintive precatory exclamation, equivalent to "my dear lady."

You might have spoken a thousand things that would
Have done the time more benefit and graced
Your kindness better.
PAUL.   You are one of those
Would have him wed again.
DION.   If you would not so,
You pity not the state, nor the remembrance
Of his most sovereign name; consider little
What dangers, by his highness' fail of issue,
May drop upon his kingdom and devour
Incertain lookers on.[4] What were more holy
Than to rejoice the former queen is well?[5]
What holier than, for royalty's repair,
For present comfort and for future good,
To bless the bed of majesty again
With a sweet fellow to 't?
PAUL.   There is none worthy,
Respecting her[6] that 's gone. Besides, the gods
Will have fulfill'd their secret purposes;
For has not the divine Apollo said,
Is 't not the tenor of his oracle,
That King Leontes shall not have an heir
Till his lost child be found? which that it shall,
Is all as monstrous to our human reason
As my Antigonus to break his grave
And come again to me; who, on my life,
Did perish with the infant. 'T is your counsel
My lord should to the heavens be contrary,
Oppose against their wills. [*To* LEONTES] Care not for issue;
The crown will find an heir: great Alexander
Left his to the worthiest; so his successor
Was like to be the best.
LEON.   Good Paulina,
Who hast the memory of Hermione,
I know, in honour, O, that ever I
Had squared me to thy counsel!—then, even now,
I might have look'd upon my queen's full eyes;
Have taken treasure from her lips,—
PAUL.   And left them

---

[4]*Incertain lookers on*] Perplexed bystanders, mere spectators, who would not know what course to take in case of revolution.
[5]*well*] happy, at rest.
[6]*Respecting her*] If we take her into consideration.

   More rich for what they yielded.
LEON.   Thou speak'st truth.
   No more such wives; therefore, no wife: one worse,
   And better used, would make her sainted spirit
   Again possess her corpse, and on this stage,
   Where we offenders now, appear[7] soul-vex'd,
   And begin, "Why to me?"[8]
PAUL.   Had she such power,
   She had just cause.
LEON.   She had; and would incense me
   To murder her I married.
PAUL.   I should so.
   Were I the ghost that walk'd, I 'ld bid you mark
   Her eye, and tell me for what dull part in 't
   You chose her; then I 'ld shriek, that even your ears
   Should rift to hear me; and the words that follow'd
   Should be "Remember mine."[9]
LEON.   Stars, stars,
   And all eyes else dead coals! Fear thou no wife;
   I 'll have no wife, Paulina.
PAUL.   Will you swear
   Never to marry but by my free leave?
LEON. Never, Paulina; so be blest my spirit!
PAUL. Then, good my lords, bear witness to his oath.
CLEO. You tempt him over-much.
PAUL.   Unless another,
   As like Hermione as is her picture,
   Affront[10] his eye.
CLEO.   Good madam,—
PAUL.   I have done.
   Yet, if my lord will marry,—if you will, sir,
   No remedy, but you will,—give me the office
   To choose you a queen: she shall not be so young
   As was your former; but she shall be such
   As, walk'd your first queen's ghost, it should take joy
   To see her in your arms.
LEON.   My true Paulina,

[7]*Where we offenders now, appear*] The verb "are" is here understood after "we." "We"
is equivalent to "we 're." The Folios disarranged the words thus: (*Where we Offendors
now appeare*). More violent changes than that adopted in the text have been suggested; none are satisfactory.
[8]"*Why to me?*"] Why did you mete out this treatment to me?
[9]"*Remember mine*"] "Remember my eyes."
[10]*Affront*] Confront.

We shall not marry till thou bid'st us.

PAUL.   That
    Shall be when your first queen 's again in breath;
    Never till then.

Enter a Gentleman

GENT.   One that gives out himself Prince Florizel,
    Son of Polixenes, with his princess, she
    The fairest I have yet beheld, desires access
    To your high presence.

LEON.   What with him? he comes not
    Like to his father's greatness: his approach,
    So out of circumstance[11] and sudden, tells us
    'T is not a visitation framed, but forced
    By need and accident. What train?

GENT.   But few,
    And those but mean.

LEON.   His princess, say you, with him?

GENT.   Ay, the most peerless piece of earth, I think,
    That e'er the sun shone bright on.

PAUL.   O Hermione,
    As every present time doth boast itself
    Above a better gone, so must thy grave[12]
    Give way to what 's seen now! Sir, you yourself
    Have said and writ so, but your writing now
    Is colder than that theme, "She had not been,
    Nor was not to be equall'd;"—thus your verse
    Flow'd with her beauty once: 't is shrewdly ebb'd,[13]
    To say you have seen a better.

GENT.   Pardon, madam:
    The one I have almost forgot,—your pardon,—
    The other, when she has obtain'd your eye,
    Will have your tongue too. This is a creature,
    Would she begin a sect, might quench the zeal
    Of all professors else;[14] make proselytes
    Of who she but bid follow.

PAUL.   How! not women?

GENT.   Women will love her, that she is a woman
    More worth than any man; men, that she is

---

[11]*out of circumstance*] without ceremony.
[12]*thy grave*] all that is buried in thy grave, thy beauty.
[13]'*t is shrewdly ebb'd*] 't is a sad decline.
[14]*all professors else*] all who profess another faith.

The rarest of all women.
LEON.   Go, Cleomenes;
Yourself, assisted with your honour'd friends,
Bring them to our embracement.

                    [*Exeunt* CLEOMENES *and others*.

                    Still, 't is strange
He thus should steal upon us.
PAUL.   Had our prince,
Jewel of children, seen this hour, he had pair'd
Well with this lord: there was not full a month
Between their births.
LEON.   Prithee, no more; cease; thou know'st
He dies to me again when talk'd of: sure,
When I shall see this gentleman, thy speeches
Will bring me to consider that which may
Unfurnish me of reason. They are come.

Re-enter CLEOMENES *and others, with* FLORIZEL *and* PERDITA

Your mother was most true to wedlock, prince;
For she did print your royal father off,
Conceiving you: were I but twenty one,
Your father's image is so hit in you,
His very air, that I should call you brother,
As I did him, and speak of something wildly
By us perform'd before. Most dearly welcome!
And your fair princess,—goddess!—O, alas!
I lost a couple, that 'twixt heaven and earth
Might thus have stood begetting wonder, as
You, gracious couple, do: and then I lost,
All mine own folly, the society,
Amity too, of your brave father, whom,
Though bearing misery, I desire my life
Once more to look on him.
FLO.   By his command
Have I here touch'd Sicilia, and from him
Give you all greetings, that a king, at friend,[15]
Can send his brother: and, but infirmity,
Which waits upon worn times,[16] hath something seized
His wish'd ability, he had himself
The lands and waters 'twixt your throne and his

[15]*at friend*] on terms of friendship.
[16]*worn times*] wasting years.

Measured to look upon you; whom he loves,
He bade me say so, more than all the sceptres
And those that bear them living.

LEON.   O my brother,
Good gentleman! the wrongs I have done thee stir
Afresh within me; and these thy offices,
So rarely kind, are as interpreters
Of my behind-hand slackness! Welcome hither,
As is the spring to the earth. And hath he too
Exposed this paragon to the fearful usage,
At least ungentle, of the dreadful Neptune,
To greet a man not worth her pains, much less
The adventure of her person?

FLO.   Good my lord,
She came from Libya.

LEON.   Where the warlike Smalus,
That noble honour'd lord, is fear'd and loved?

FLO.   Most royal sir, from thence; from him, whose daughter
His tears proclaim'd his, parting with her: thence,
A prosperous south-wind friendly, we have cross'd,
To execute the charge my father gave me,
For visiting your highness: my best train
I have from your Sicilian shores dismiss'd;
Who for Bohemia bend, to signify
Not only my success in Libya, sir,
But my arrival, and my wife's, in safety
Here where we are.

LEON.   The blessed gods
Purge all infection from our air whilst you
Do climate[17] here! You have a holy[18] father,
A graceful gentleman; against whose person,
So sacred as it is, I have done sin:
For which the heavens, taking angry note,
Have left me issueless; and your father 's blest,
As he from heaven merits it, with you
Worthy his goodness. What might I have been,
Might I a son and daughter now have look'd on,
Such goodly things as you!

Enter a Lord

LORD.   Most noble sir,

---

[17]*climate*] sojourn.
[18]*holy*] just, good.

That which I shall report will bear no credit,
Were not the proof so nigh. Please you, great sir,
Bohemia greets you from himself by me;
Desires you to attach his son, who has—
His dignity and duty both cast off—
Fled from his father, from his hopes, and with
A shepherd's daughter.

LEON.   Where 's Bohemia? speak.

LORD.   Here in your city; I now came from him:
I speak amazedly; and it becomes
My marvel and my message. To your court
Whiles he was hastening, in the chase, it seems,
Of this fair couple, meets he on the way
The father of this seeming lady and
Her brother, having both their country quitted
With this young prince.

FLO.   Camillo has betray'd me;
Whose honour and whose honesty till now
Endured all weathers.

LORD.   Lay 't so to his charge:
He 's with the king your father.

LEON.   Who? Camillo?

LORD.   Camillo, sir; I spake with him; who now
Has these poor men in question.[19] Never saw I
Wretches so quake: they kneel, they kiss the earth;
Forswear themselves as often as they speak:
Bohemia stops his ears, and threatens them
With divers deaths in death.

PER.   O my poor father!
The heaven sets spies upon us, will not have
Our contract celebrated.

LEON.   You are married?

FLO.   We are not, sir, nor are we like to be;
The stars, I see, will kiss the valleys first:
The odds for high and low 's alike.[20]

LEON.   My lord,
Is this the daughter of a king?

FLO.   She is,
When once she is my wife.

LEON.   That "once," I see by your good father's speed,
Will come on very slowly. I am sorry,

---

[19]*in question*] under examination, in conversation.
[20]*The odds for high and low 's alike*] High-born and low-born have the same chances.

Most sorry, you have broken from his liking
Where you were tied in duty, and as sorry
Your choice is not so rich in worth as beauty,
That you might well enjoy her.

FLO.   Dear, look up:
Though Fortune, visible an enemy,
Should chase us with my father, power no jot
Hath she to change our loves. Beseech you, sir,
Remember since[21] you owed no more to time
Than I do now: with thought of such affections,
Step forth mine advocate; at your request
My father will grant precious things as trifles.

LEON.   Would he do so, I 'ld beg your precious mistress,
Which he counts but a trifle.

PAUL.   Sir, my liege,
Your eye hath too much youth in 't: not a month
'Fore your queen died, she was more worth such gazes
Than what you look on now.

LEON.   I thought of her,
Even in these looks I made. [*To* FLORIZEL] But your petition
Is yet unanswer'd. I will to your father:
Your honour not o'erthrown by your desires,
I am friend to them and you: upon which errand
I now go toward him; therefore follow me
And mark what way I make: come, good my lord.   [*Exeunt.*

SCENE II. *Before Leontes' Palace*

Enter AUTOLYCUS *and a* Gentleman

AUT.   Beseech you, sir, were you present at this relation?

FIRST GENT.   I was by at the opening of the fardel, heard the old shepherd deliver the manner how he found it: whereupon, after a little amazedness, we were all commanded out of the chamber; only
this methought I heard the shepherd say, he found the child.

AUT.   I would most gladly know the issue of it.

FIRST GENT.   I make a broken delivery[1] of the business; but the
changes I perceived in the king and Camillo were very notes of admiration: they seemed almost, with staring on one another, to tear

---

[21]*since*] the time when.

---

[1]*broken delivery*] fragmentary account.

ACT V, SCENE II

the cases of their eyes; there was speech in their dumbness, language in their very gesture; they looked as they had heard of a world ransomed, or one destroyed: a notable passion of wonder appeared in them; but the wisest beholder, that knew no more but seeing, could not say if the importance[2] were joy or sorrow; but in the extremity of the one,[3] it must needs be.

Enter another Gentleman

Here comes a gentleman that haply knows more. The news, Rogero?

SEC. GENT.   Nothing but bonfires: the oracle is fulfilled; the king's daughter is found: such a deal of wonder is broken out within this hour, that ballad-makers cannot be able to express it.

Enter a third Gentleman

Here comes the Lady Paulina's steward: he can deliver you more. How goes it now, sir? this news which is called true is so like an old tale, that the verity of it is in strong suspicion: has the king found his heir?

THIRD GENT.   Most true, if ever truth were pregnant by circumstance:[4] that which you hear you 'll swear you see, there is such unity in the proofs. The mantle of Queen Hermione's, her jewel about the neck of it, the letters of Antigonus found with it, which they know to be his character,[5] the majesty of the creature in resemblance of the mother, the affection[6] of nobleness which nature shows above her breeding, and many other evidences proclaim her with all certainty to be the king's daughter. Did you see the meeting of the two kings?

SEC. GENT.   No.

THIRD GENT.   Then have you lost a sight, which was to be seen, cannot be spoken of. There might you have beheld one joy crown another, so and in such manner, that it seemed sorrow wept to take leave of them, for their joy waded in tears. There was casting up of eyes, holding up of hands, with countenance of such distraction, that they were to be known by garment, not by favour. Our king, being ready to leap out of himself for joy of his found daughter, as if that joy were now become a loss, cries "O, thy mother, thy mother!" then asks Bohemia forgiveness; then embraces his

---

[2]*importance*] import, purport.
[3]*the one*] either one.
[4]*pregnant by circumstance*] convincing through corroborative detail.
[5]*character*] handwriting.
[6]*affection*] disposition or quality.

son-in-law; then again worries he his daughter with clipping[7] her; now he thanks the old shepherd, which stands by like a weather-bitten conduit[8] of many kings' reigns. I never heard of such another encounter, which lames report to follow it and undoes description to do it.

SEC. GENT.   What, pray you, became of Antigonus, that carried hence the child?

THIRD GENT.   Like an old tale still, which will have matter to rehearse, though credit be asleep and not an ear open. He was torn to pieces with a bear:[9] this avouches[10] the shepherd's son; who has not only his innocence, which seems much, to justify him, but a handkerchief and rings of his that Paulina knows.

FIRST GENT.   What became of his bark and his followers?

THIRD GENT.   Wrecked the same instant of their master's death and in the view of the shepherd: so that all the instruments which aided to expose the child were even then lost when it was found. But O, the noble combat that 'twixt joy and sorrow was fought in Paulina! She had one eye declined for the loss of her husband, another elevated that the oracle was fulfilled: she lifted the princess from the earth, and so locks her in embracing, as if she would pin her to her heart that she might no more be in danger of losing.

FIRST GENT.   The dignity of this act was worth the audience of kings and princes; for by such was it acted.

THIRD GENT.   One of the prettiest touches of all and that which angled for mine eyes, caught the water though not the fish,[11] was when, at the relation of the queen's death, with the manner how she came to 't bravely confessed and lamented by the king, how attentiveness wounded his daughter; till, from one sign of dolour to another, she did, with an "Alas," I would fain say, bleed tears, for I am sure my heart wept blood. Who was most marble[12] there changed colour; some swooned, all sorrowed: if all the world could have seen 't, the woe had been universal.

FIRST GENT.   Are they returned to the court?

THIRD GENT.   No: the princess hearing of her mother's statue, which is in the keeping of Paulina,—a piece many years in doing and

---

[7]*clipping*] embracing.

[8]*weather-bitten conduit*] a fountain bitten or corroded by the weather. Fountains were often made of bronze or marble, shaped like human figures.

[9]*with a bear*] by a bear.

[10]*avouches*] corroborates.

[11]*caught . . . fish*] A very stilted conceit, characteristic of much Elizabethan writing.

[12]*most marble*] most hardened.

now newly performed by that rare Italian master, Julio Romano,[13] who, had he himself eternity and could put breath into his work, would beguile Nature of her custom,[14] so perfectly he is her ape: he so near to Hermione hath done Hermione, that they say one would speak to her and stand in hope of answer:—thither with all greediness of affection are they gone, and there they intend to sup.

SEC. GENT.   I thought she had some great matter there in hand; for she hath privately twice or thrice a day, ever since the death of Hermione, visited that removed house. Shall we thither and with our company piece[15] the rejoicing?

FIRST GENT.   Who would be thence that has the benefit of access? every wink of an eye, some new grace will be born: our absence makes us unthrifty to our knowledge. Let 's along.

[Exeunt Gentlemen.

AUT.   Now, had I not the dash of my former life in me, would preferment drop on my head. I brought the old man and his son aboard the prince;[16] told him I heard them talk of a fardel and I know not what: but he at that time, overfond of the shepherd's daughter, so he then took her to be, who began to be much sea-sick, and himself little better, extremity of weather continuing, this mystery remained undiscovered. But 't is all one to me; for had I been the finder out of this secret, it would not have relished[17] among my other discredits.

Enter Shepherd *and* Clown

Here come those I have done good to against my will, and already appearing in the blossoms of their fortune.

SHEP.   Come, boy; I am past moe children, but thy sons and daughters will be all gentlemen born.

CLO.   You are well met, sir. You denied to fight with me this other day, because I was no gentleman born. See you these clothes? say you see them not and think me still no gentleman born: you were best say these robes are not gentlemen born: give me the lie, do, and try whether I am not now a gentleman born.

[13]*Julio Romano*] Julio Romano (1492–1546) is well known as a painter and architect. But Vasari, the sixteenth-century biographer of Italian artists, quotes an epitaph on Romano, which credits him with skill in sculpture in addition.

[14]*would beguile . . . custom*] would draw Nature's customers from her and attract them to himself.

[15]*piece*] contribute to.

[16]*aboard the prince*] aboard the prince's ship.

[17]*relished*] found appreciation, been valued.

AUT.   I know you are now, sir, a gentleman born.

CLO.   Ay, and have been so any time these four hours.

SHEP.   And so have I, boy.

CLO.   So you have: but I was a gentleman born before my father; for the king's son took me by the hand, and called me brother; and then the two kings called my father brother; and then the prince my brother and the princess my sister called my father father; and so we wept, and there was the first gentleman-like tears that ever we shed.

SHEP.   We may live, son, to shed many more.

CLO.   Ay; or else 't were hard luck, being in so preposterous estate[18] as we are.

AUT.   I humbly beseech you, sir, to pardon me all the faults I have committed to your worship, and to give me your good report to the prince my master.

SHEP.   Prithee, son, do; for we must be gentle, now we are gentlemen.

CLO.   Thou wilt amend thy life?

AUT.   Ay, an it like your good worship.

CLO.   Give me thy hand: I will swear to the prince thou art as honest a true fellow as any is in Bohemia.

SHEP.   You may say it, but not swear it.

CLO.   Not swear it, now I am a gentleman? Let boors and franklins[19] say it, I 'll swear it.

SHEP.   How if it be false, son?

CLO.   If it be ne'er so false, a true gentleman may swear it in the behalf of his friend: and I 'll swear to the prince thou art a tall fellow of thy hands[20] and that thou wilt not be drunk; but I know thou art no tall fellow of thy hands and that thou wilt be drunk: but I 'll swear it, and I would thou wouldst be a tall fellow of thy hands.

AUT.   I will prove so, sir, to my power.

CLO.   Ay, by any means prove a tall fellow: if I do not wonder how thou darest venture to be drunk, not being a tall fellow, trust me not. Hark! the kings and the princes, our kindred, are going to see the queen's picture. Come, follow us: we 'll be thy good masters.[21]

[*Exeunt.*

---

[18]*preposterous estate*] prosperous state; "preposterous" is the clown's blunder.

[19]*franklins*] freemen, freeholders, below the rank of gentlemen.

[20]*a tall fellow of thy hands*] a brave man, a man of notable valour. "Tall" is often used in the sense of bold or courageous, as it appears later. Cotgrave, *Fr.-Engl. Dict.*, 1611, defines "homme à la main" as "a man of execution or valour; *a man of his hands*."

[21]*good masters*] generous patrons.

SCENE III. *A Chapel in Paulina's House*

Enter LEONTES, POLIXENES, FLORIZEL, PERDITA, CAMILLO, PAULINA,
Lords, *and* Attendants

LEON.   O grave and good Paulina, the great comfort
    That I have had of thee!
PAUL.   What, sovereign sir,
    I did not well, I meant well. All my services
    You have paid home: but that you have vouchsafed
    With your crown'd brother and these your contracted
    Heirs of your kingdoms, my poor house to visit,
    It is a surplus of your grace, which never
    My life may last to answer.
LEON.   O Paulina,
    We honour you with trouble:[1] but we came
    To see the statue of our queen: your gallery
    Have we pass'd through, not without much content
    In many singularities; but we saw not
    That which my daughter came to look upon,
    The statue of her mother.
PAUL.   As she lived peerless,
    So her dead likeness, I do well believe,
    Excels whatever yet you look'd upon
    Or hand of man hath done; therefore I keep it
    Lonely,[2] apart. But here it is: prepare
    To see the life as lively mock'd as ever
    Still sleep mock'd death: behold, and say 't is well.
               [PAULINA *draws a curtain, and discovers*
                  HERMIONE *standing like a statue.*
    I like your silence, it the more shows off
    Your wonder: but yet speak; first, you, my liege.
    Comes it not something near?
LEON.   Her natural posture!
    Chide me, dear stone, that I may say indeed
    Thou art Hermione; or rather, thou art she
    In thy not chiding, for she was as tender
    As infancy and grace. But yet, Paulina,
    Hermione was not so much wrinkled, nothing
    So aged as this seems.

---

[1]*We . . . trouble*] The honour we pay you gives you trouble.
[2]*Lonely*] This is Hanmer's correction of the Folio reading *Louely*, or *Lovely*, which has
been interpreted as "lovingly," "with more than ordinary tenderness." "Lonely, apart"
is tautological. The Folio reading seems defensible.

POL.   O, not by much.

PAUL.   So much the more our carver's excellence;
     Which lets go by some sixteen years and makes her
     As she lived[3] now.

LEON.   As now she might have done,
     So much to my good comfort, as it is
     Now piercing to my soul. O, thus she stood,
     Even with such life of majesty, warm life.
     As now it coldly stands, when first I woo'd her!
     I am ashamed: does not the stone rebuke me
     For being more stone than it? O royal piece,
     There 's magic in thy majesty, which has
     My evils conjured to remembrance, and
     From thy admiring daughter took the spirits,
     Standing like stone with thee.

PER.   And give me leave,
     And do not say 't is superstition, that
     I kneel and then implore her blessing. Lady,
     Dear queen, that ended when I but began,
     Give me that hand of yours to kiss.

PAUL.   O, patience!
     The statue is but newly fix'd, the colour 's
     Not dry.

CAM.   My lord, your sorrow was too sore laid on,
     Which sixteen winters cannot blow away,
     So many summers dry: scarce any joy
     Did ever so long live; no sorrow
     But kill'd itself much sooner.

POL.   Dear my brother,
     Let him that was the cause of this have power
     To take off so much grief from you as he
     Will piece up in himself.[4]

PAUL.   Indeed, my lord,
     If I had thought the sight of my poor image
     Would thus have wrought you, for the stone is mine,
     I 'ld not have show'd it.

LEON.   Do not draw the curtain.

PAUL.   No longer shall you gaze on 't, lest your fancy
     May think anon it moves.

LEON.   Let be, let be.

---

[3]*As she lived*] As if she lived.
[4]*Will piece up in himself*] Will make his own, take upon himself.

Would I were dead, but that, methinks, already—[5]
What was he that did make it? See, my lord,
Would you not deem it breathed? and that those veins
Did verily bear blood?
POL.   Masterly done:
The very life seems warm upon her lip.
LEON.   The fixure[6] of her eye has motion in 't,
As we are mock'd with art.[7]
PAUL.   I 'll draw the curtain:
My lord 's almost so far transported that
He 'll think anon it lives.
LEON.   O sweet Paulina,
Make me to think so twenty years together!
No settled senses of the world can match
The pleasure of that madness. Let 't alone.
PAUL.   I am sorry, sir, I have thus far stirr'd you: but
I could afflict you farther.
LEON.   Do, Paulina;
For this affliction has a taste as sweet
As any cordial comfort. Still, methinks,
There is an air comes from her: what fine chisel
Could ever yet cut breath? Let no man mock me,
For I will kiss her.
PAUL.   Good my lord, forbear:
The ruddiness upon her lip is wet;
You 'll mar it if you kiss it, stain your own
With oily painting. Shall I draw the curtain?
LEON.   No, not these twenty years.
PER.   So long could I
Stand by, a looker on.
PAUL.   Either forbear,
Quit presently the chapel, or resolve you[8]
For more amazement. If you can behold it,
I 'll make the statue move indeed, descend
And take you by the hand: but then you 'll think,
Which I protest against, I am assisted
By wicked powers.

---

[5]*Would I were dead, . . . already—*] The interrupted sentence means, "May I die, if I did
not think this statue already moved."
[6]*fixure*] fixity, fixedness, stability.
[7]*As we are mock'd with art*] For so we are mocked by art.
[8]*Either forbear . . . resolve you*] Either abstain from touching, and at once quit the
chapel, or make up your mind.

LEON.　　　　　　　　What you can make her do,
　　I am content to look on: what to speak,
　　I am content to hear; for 't is as easy
　　To make her speak as move.
PAUL.　　　　　　　　　　It is required
　　You do awake your faith. Then all stand still;
　　On: those[9] that think it is unlawful business
　　I am about, let them depart.
LEON.　　　　　　　　Proceed:
　　No foot shall stir.
PAUL.　　　　　　　Music, awake her; strike!　　　　　[*Music.*
　　'T is time; descend; be stone no more; approach;
　　Strike all that look upon[10] with marvel. Come,
　　I 'll fill your grave up: stir, nay, come away,
　　Bequeath to death your numbness, for from him
　　Dear life redeems you. You perceive she stirs:
　　　　　　　　　　　　　[HERMIONE *comes down.*
　　Start not; her actions shall be holy as
　　You hear my spell is lawful: do not shun her
　　Until you see her die again; for then
　　You kill her double. Nay, present your hand:
　　When she was young you woo'd her; now in age
　　Is she become the suitor?
LEON.　　　　　　　　　O, she 's warm!
　　If this be magic, let it be an art
　　Lawful as eating.
POL.　　　　　She embraces him.
CAM.　　She hangs about his neck:
　　If she pertain to life let her speak too.
POL.　　Ay, and make 't manifest where she has lived,
　　Or how stolen from the dead.
PAUL.　　　　　　　　That she is living,
　　Were it but told you, should be hooted at
　　Like an old tale: but it appears she lives,
　　Though yet she speak not. Mark a little while.
　　Please you to interpose, fair madam: kneel
　　And pray your mother's blessing. Turn, good lady;
　　Our Perdita is found.
HER.　　　　　　　You gods, look down,
　　And from your sacred vials pour your graces
　　Upon my daughter's head! Tell me, mine own,

---

[9]*On: those*] Thus the Folios. Hanmer substituted *Or those*, a welcome simplification.
[10]*look upon*] look on.

Where hast thou been preserved? where lived? how found
Thy father's court? for thou shalt hear that I,
Knowing by Paulina that the oracle
Gave hope thou wast in being, have preserved
Myself to see the issue.

PAUL.   There 's time enough for that;
Lest they desire upon this push[11] to trouble
Your joys with like relation. Go together,
You precious winners all; your exultation
Partake to every one. I, an old turtle,
Will wing me to some wither'd bough and there
My mate, that 's never to be found again,
Lament till I am lost.[12]

LEON.   O, peace, Paulina!
Thou shouldst a husband take by my consent,
As I by thine a wife: this is a match,
And made between 's by vows. Thou hast found mine;
But how, is to be question'd; for I saw her,
As I thought, dead; and have in vain said many
A prayer upon her grave. I 'll not seek far,—
For him, I partly know his mind,—to find thee
An honourable husband. Come, Camillo,
And take her by the hand, whose[13] worth and honesty
Is richly noted and here justified
By us, a pair of kings. Let 's from this place.
What! look upon my brother: both your pardons,
That e'er I put between your holy looks
My ill suspicion. This your son-in-law,
And son unto the king, whom heavens directing,[14]
Is troth-plight to your daughter. Good Paulina,
Lead us from hence, where we may leisurely
Each one demand, and answer to his part
Perform'd in this wide gap of time, since first
We were dissever'd: hastily lead away.   [*Exeunt.*

---

[11]*this push*] this emergency.
[12]*lost*] given up (to death).
[13]*whose*] The antecedent is "Camillo."
[14]*This your son-in-law, . . . directing*] Thus the Folios. The irregularities of the grammatical construction here are removed by reading *This is* for *This*, and *who* for *whom*.
But a gesture might well supply *is* after *this*, and *whom heaven 's directing* (*i.e.*, who
under heaven's direction) is a grammatical solecism of a kind which is *familiar* in
Shakespeare's work.

DOVER · THRIFT · EDITIONS

POETRY

A Shropshire Lad, A. E. Housman. 64pp. 26468-8 $1.00

Lyric Poems, John Keats. 80pp. 26871-3 $1.00

Gunga Din and Other Favorite Poems, Rudyard Kipling. 80pp. 26471-8 $1.00

The Congo and Other Poems, Vachel Lindsay. 96pp. 27272-9 $1.50

Evangeline and Other Poems, Henry Wadsworth Longfellow. 64pp. 28255-4 $1.00

Favorite Poems, Henry Wadsworth Longfellow. 96pp. 27273-7 $1.00

"To His Coy Mistress" and Other Poems, Andrew Marvell. 64pp. 29544-3 $1.00

Spoon River Anthology, Edgar Lee Masters. 144pp. 27275-3 $1.50

Renascence and Other Poems, Edna St. Vincent Millay. 64pp. (Available in U.S. only.) 26873-X $1.00

Selected Poems, John Milton. 128pp. 27554-X $1.50

Civil War Poetry: An Anthology, Paul Negri (ed.). 128pp. 29883-3 $1.50

English Victorian Poetry: An Anthology, Paul Negri (ed.). 256pp. 40425-0 $2.00

Great Sonnets, Paul Negri (ed.). 96pp. 28052-7 $1.00

The Raven and Other Favorite Poems, Edgar Allan Poe. 64pp. 26685-0 $1.00

Essay on Man and Other Poems, Alexander Pope. 128pp. 28053-5 $1.50

Early Poems, Ezra Pound. 80pp. (Available in U.S. only.) 28745-9 $1.00

Great Poems by American Women: An Anthology, Susan L. Rattiner (ed.). 224pp. (Available in U.S. only.) 40164-2 $2.00

Little Orphant Annie and Other Poems, James Whitcomb Riley. 80pp. 28260-0 $1.00

"Miniver Cheevy" and Other Poems, Edwin Arlington Robinson. 64pp. 28756-4 $1.00

Goblin Market and Other Poems, Christina Rossetti. 64pp. 28055-1 $1.00

Chicago Poems, Carl Sandburg. 80pp. 28057-8 $1.00

The Shooting of Dan McGrew and Other Poems, Robert Service. 96pp. (Available in U.S. only.) 27556-6 $1.50

Complete Sonnets, William Shakespeare. 80pp. 26686-9 $1.00

Selected Poems, Percy Bysshe Shelley. 128pp. 27558-2 $1.50

African-American Poetry: An Anthology, 1773–1930, Joan R. Sherman (ed.). 96pp. 29604-0 $1.00

100 Best-Loved Poems, Philip Smith (ed.). 96pp. 28553-7 $1.00

Native American Songs and Poems: An Anthology, Brian Swann (ed.). 64pp. 29450-1 $1.00

Selected Poems, Alfred Lord Tennyson. 112pp. 27282-6 $1.50

Aeneid, Vergil (Publius Vergilius Maro). 256pp. 28749-1 $2.00

Christmas Carols: Complete Verses, Shane Weller (ed.). 64pp. 27397-0 $1.00

Great Love Poems, Shane Weller (ed.). 128pp. 27284-2 $1.00

Civil War Poetry and Prose, Walt Whitman. 96pp. 28507-3 $1.00

Selected Poems, Walt Whitman. 128pp. 26878-0 $1.00

The Ballad of Reading Gaol and Other Poems, Oscar Wilde. 64pp. 27072-6 $1.00

Early Poems, William Carlos Williams. 64pp. (Available in U.S. only.) 29294-0 $1.00

Favorite Poems, William Wordsworth. 80pp. 27073-4 $1.00

World War One British Poets: Brooke, Owen, Sassoon, Rosenberg, and Others, Candace Ward (ed.). (Available in U.S. only.) 29568-0 $1.00

Early Poems, William Butler Yeats. 128pp. 27808-5 $1.50

"Easter, 1916" and Other Poems, William Butler Yeats. 80pp. (Available in U.S. only.) 29771-3 $1.00

DOVER · THRIFT · EDITIONS

FICTION

FLATLAND: A ROMANCE OF MANY DIMENSIONS, Edwin A. Abbott. 96pp. 27263-X $1.00

SHORT STORIES, Louisa May Alcott. 64pp. 29063-8 $1.00

WINESBURG, OHIO, Sherwood Anderson. 160pp. 28269-4 $2.00

PERSUASION, Jane Austen. 224pp. 29555-9 $2.00

PRIDE AND PREJUDICE, Jane Austen. 272pp. 28473-5 $2.00

SENSE AND SENSIBILITY, Jane Austen. 272pp. 29049-2 $2.00

LOOKING BACKWARD, Edward Bellamy. 160pp. 29038-7 $2.00

BEOWULF, Beowulf (trans. by R. K. Gordon). 64pp. 27264-8 $1.00

CIVIL WAR STORIES, Ambrose Bierce. 128pp. 28038-1 $1.00

"THE MOONLIT ROAD" AND OTHER GHOST AND HORROR STORIES, Ambrose Bierce (John Grafton, ed.) 96pp. 40056-5 $1.00

WUTHERING HEIGHTS, Emily Brontë. 256pp. 29256-8 $2.00

THE THIRTY-NINE STEPS, John Buchan. 96pp. 28201-5 $1.50

TARZAN OF THE APES, Edgar Rice Burroughs. 224pp. (Available in U.S. only.) 29570-2 $2.00

ALICE'S ADVENTURES IN WONDERLAND, Lewis Carroll. 96pp. 27543-4 $1.00

THROUGH THE LOOKING-GLASS, Lewis Carroll. 128pp. 40878-7 $1.50

MY ÁNTONIA, Willa Cather. 176pp. 28240-6 $2.00

O PIONEERS!, Willa Cather. 128pp. 27785-2 $1.00

PAUL'S CASE AND OTHER STORIES, Willa Cather. 64pp. 29057-3 $1.00

FIVE GREAT SHORT STORIES, Anton Chekhov. 96pp. 26463-7 $1.00

TALES OF CONJURE AND THE COLOR LINE, Charles Waddell Chesnutt. 128pp. 40426-9 $1.50

FAVORITE FATHER BROWN STORIES, G. K. Chesterton. 96pp. 27545-0 $1.00

THE AWAKENING, Kate Chopin. 128pp. 27786-0 $1.00

A PAIR OF SILK STOCKINGS AND OTHER STORIES, Kate Chopin. 64pp. 29264-9 $1.00

HEART OF DARKNESS, Joseph Conrad. 80pp. 26464-5 $1.00

LORD JIM, Joseph Conrad. 256pp. 40650-4 $2.00

THE SECRET SHARER AND OTHER STORIES, Joseph Conrad. 128pp. 27546-9 $1.00

THE "LITTLE REGIMENT" AND OTHER CIVIL WAR STORIES, Stephen Crane. 80pp. 29557-5 $1.00

THE OPEN BOAT AND OTHER STORIES, Stephen Crane. 128pp. 27547-7 $1.50

THE RED BADGE OF COURAGE, Stephen Crane. 112pp. 26465-3 $1.00

MOLL FLANDERS, Daniel Defoe. 256pp. 29093-X $2.00

ROBINSON CRUSOE, Daniel Defoe. 288pp. 40427-7 $2.00

A CHRISTMAS CAROL, Charles Dickens. 80pp. 26865-9 $1.00

THE CRICKET ON THE HEARTH AND OTHER CHRISTMAS STORIES, Charles Dickens. 128pp. 28039-X $1.00

A TALE OF TWO CITIES, Charles Dickens. 304pp. 40651-2 $2.00

THE DOUBLE, Fyodor Dostoyevsky. 128pp. 29572-9 $1.50

THE GAMBLER, Fyodor Dostoyevsky. 112pp. 29081-6 $1.50

NOTES FROM THE UNDERGROUND, Fyodor Dostoyevsky. 96pp. 27053-X $1.00

THE ADVENTURE OF THE DANCING MEN AND OTHER STORIES, Sir Arthur Conan Doyle. 80pp. 29558-3 $1.00

THE HOUND OF THE BASKERVILLES, Arthur Conan Doyle. 128pp. 28214-7 $1.50

THE LOST WORLD, Arthur Conan Doyle. 176pp. 40060-3 $1.50

DOVER·THRIFT·EDITIONS

FICTION

SIX GREAT SHERLOCK HOLMES STORIES, Sir Arthur Conan Doyle. 112pp. 27055-6 $1.00

SILAS MARNER, George Eliot. 160pp. 29246-0 $1.50

THIS SIDE OF PARADISE, F. Scott Fitzgerald. 208pp. 28999-0 $2.00

"THE DIAMOND AS BIG AS THE RITZ" AND OTHER STORIES, F. Scott Fitzgerald. 29991-0 $2.00

THE REVOLT OF "MOTHER" AND OTHER STORIES, Mary E. Wilkins Freeman. 128pp. 40428-5 $1.50

MADAME BOVARY, Gustave Flaubert. 256pp. 29257-6 $2.00

WHERE ANGELS FEAR TO TREAD, E. M. Forster. 128pp. (Available in U.S. only.) 27791-7 $1.50

A ROOM WITH A VIEW, E. M. Forster. 176pp. (Available in U.S. only.) 28467-0 $2.00

THE IMMORALIST, André Gide. 112pp. (Available in U.S. only.) 29237-1 $1.50

"THE YELLOW WALLPAPER" AND OTHER STORIES, Charlotte Perkins Gilman. 80pp. 29857-4 $1.00

HERLAND, Charlotte Perkins Gilman. 128pp. 40429-3 $1.50

THE OVERCOAT AND OTHER STORIES, Nikolai Gogol. 112pp. 27057-2 $1.50

GREAT GHOST STORIES, John Grafton (ed.). 112pp. 27270-2 $1.00

DETECTION BY GASLIGHT, Douglas G. Greene (ed.). 272pp. 29928-7 $2.00

THE MABINOGION, Lady Charlotte E. Guest. 192pp. 29541-9 $2.00

"THE FIDDLER OF THE REELS" AND OTHER SHORT STORIES, Thomas Hardy. 80pp. 29960-0 $1.50

THE LUCK OF ROARING CAMP AND OTHER STORIES, Bret Harte. 96pp. 27271-0 $1.00

THE SCARLET LETTER, Nathaniel Hawthorne. 192pp. 28048-9 $2.00

YOUNG GOODMAN BROWN AND OTHER STORIES, Nathaniel Hawthorne. 128pp. 27060-2 $1.00

THE GIFT OF THE MAGI AND OTHER SHORT STORIES, O. Henry. 96pp. 27061-0 $1.00

THE NUTCRACKER AND THE GOLDEN POT, E. T. A. Hoffmann. 128pp. 27806-9 $1.00

THE BEAST IN THE JUNGLE AND OTHER STORIES, Henry James. 128pp. 27552-3 $1.50

DAISY MILLER, Henry James. 64pp. 28773-4 $1.00

THE TURN OF THE SCREW, Henry James. 96pp. 26684-2 $1.00

WASHINGTON SQUARE, Henry James. 176pp. 40431-5 $2.00

THE COUNTRY OF THE POINTED FIRS, Sarah Orne Jewett. 96pp. 28196-5 $1.00

THE AUTOBIOGRAPHY OF AN EX-COLORED MAN, James Weldon Johnson. 112pp. 28512-X $1.00

DUBLINERS, James Joyce. 160pp. 26870-5 $1.00

A PORTRAIT OF THE ARTIST AS A YOUNG MAN, James Joyce. 192pp. 28050-0 $2.00

THE METAMORPHOSIS AND OTHER STORIES, Franz Kafka. 96pp. 29030-1 $1.50

THE MAN WHO WOULD BE KING AND OTHER STORIES, Rudyard Kipling. 128pp. 28051-9 $1.50

YOU KNOW ME AL, Ring Lardner. 128pp. 28513-8 $1.50

SELECTED SHORT STORIES, D. H. Lawrence. 128pp. 27794-1 $1.50

GREEN TEA AND OTHER GHOST STORIES, J. Sheridan LeFanu. 96pp. 27795-X $1.50

SHORT STORIES, Theodore Dreiser. 112pp. 28215-5 $1.50

THE CALL OF THE WILD, Jack London. 64pp. 26472-6 $1.00

FIVE GREAT SHORT STORIES, Jack London. 96pp. 27063-7 $1.00

WHITE FANG, Jack London. 160pp. 26968-X $1.00

DEATH IN VENICE, Thomas Mann. 96pp. (Available in U.S. only.) 28714-9 $1.00

IN A GERMAN PENSION: 13 Stories, Katherine Mansfield. 112pp. 28719-X $1.50

THE MOON AND SIXPENCE, W. Somerset Maugham. 176pp. (Available in U.S. only.) 28731-9 $2.00

DOVER · THRIFT · EDITIONS

FICTION

THE NECKLACE AND OTHER SHORT STORIES, Guy de Maupassant. 128pp. 27064-5 $1.00

BARTLEBY AND BENITO CERENO, Herman Melville. 112pp. 26473-4 $1.00

THE OIL JAR AND OTHER STORIES, Luigi Pirandello. 96pp. 28459-X $1.00

THE GOLD-BUG AND OTHER TALES, Edgar Allan Poe. 128pp. 26875-6 $1.00

TALES OF TERROR AND DETECTION, Edgar Allan Poe. 96pp. 28744-0 $1.00

THE QUEEN OF SPADES AND OTHER STORIES, Alexander Pushkin. 128pp. 28054-3 $1.50

SREDNI VASHTAR AND OTHER STORIES, Saki (H. H. Munro). 96pp. 28521-9 $1.00

THE STORY OF AN AFRICAN FARM, Olive Schreiner. 256pp. 40165-0 $2.00

FRANKENSTEIN, Mary Shelley. 176pp. 28211-2 $1.00

THREE LIVES, Gertrude Stein. 176pp. (Available in U.S. only.) 28059-4 $2.00

THE STRANGE CASE OF DR. JEKYLL AND MR. HYDE, Robert Louis Stevenson. 64pp. 26688-5 $1.00

TREASURE ISLAND, Robert Louis Stevenson. 160pp. 27559-0 $1.50

GULLIVER'S TRAVELS, Jonathan Swift. 240pp. 29273-8 $2.00

THE KREUTZER SONATA AND OTHER SHORT STORIES, Leo Tolstoy. 144pp. 27805-0 $1.50

THE WARDEN, Anthony Trollope. 176pp. 40076-X $2.00

FIRST LOVE AND DIARY OF A SUPERFLUOUS MAN, Ivan Turgenev. 96pp. 28775-0 $1.50

FATHERS AND SONS, Ivan Turgenev. 176pp. 40073-5 $2.00

ADVENTURES OF HUCKLEBERRY FINN, Mark Twain. 224pp. 28061-6 $2.00

THE ADVENTURES OF TOM SAWYER, Mark Twain. 192pp. 40077-8 $2.00

THE MYSTERIOUS STRANGER AND OTHER STORIES, Mark Twain. 128pp. 27069-6 $1.00

HUMOROUS STORIES AND SKETCHES, Mark Twain. 80pp. 29279-7 $1.00

CANDIDE, Voltaire (François-Marie Arouet). 112pp. 26689-3 $1.00

GREAT SHORT STORIES BY AMERICAN WOMEN, Candace Ward (ed.). 192pp. 28776-9 $2.00

"THE COUNTRY OF THE BLIND" AND OTHER SCIENCE-FICTION STORIES, H. G. Wells. 160pp. (Available in U.S. only.) 29569-9 $1.00

THE ISLAND OF DR. MOREAU, H. G. Wells. 112pp. (Available in U.S. only.) 29027-1 $1.50

THE INVISIBLE MAN, H. G. Wells. 112pp. (Available in U.S. only.) 27071-8 $1.00

THE TIME MACHINE, H. G. Wells. 80pp. (Available in U.S. only.) 28472-7 $1.00

THE WAR OF THE WORLDS, H. G. Wells. 160pp. (Available in U.S. only.) 29506-0 $1.00

ETHAN FROME, Edith Wharton. 96pp. 26690-7 $1.00

SHORT STORIES, Edith Wharton. 128pp. 28235-X $1.50

THE AGE OF INNOCENCE, Edith Wharton. 288pp. 29803-5 $2.00

THE PICTURE OF DORIAN GRAY, Oscar Wilde. 192pp. 27807-7 $1.50

JACOB'S ROOM, Virginia Woolf. 144pp. (Available in U.S. only.) 40109-X $1.50

MONDAY OR TUESDAY: Eight Stories, Virginia Woolf. 64pp. (Available in U.S. only.) 29453-6 $1.00

NONFICTION

POETICS, Aristotle. 64pp. 29577-X $1.00

NICOMACHEAN ETHICS, Aristotle. 256pp. 40096-4 $2.00

MEDITATIONS, Marcus Aurelius. 128pp. 29823-X $1.50

THE LAND OF LITTLE RAIN, Mary Austin. 96pp. 29037-0 $1.50

THE DEVIL'S DICTIONARY, Ambrose Bierce. 144pp. 27542-6 $1.00

THE ANALECTS, Confucius. 128pp. 28484-0 $2.00

CONFESSIONS OF AN ENGLISH OPIUM EATER, Thomas De Quincey. 80pp. 28742-4 $1.00

NARRATIVE OF THE LIFE OF FREDERICK DOUGLASS, Frederick Douglass. 96pp. 28499-9 $1.00